Felix O'Neill, along with his friend Dr. Garzon, investigates the chilling, ever-present and totally unexplained phenomenon of missing persons. They set out to discover why some people go missing and are never heard of again, at least in the land of the living. It may be that some of them become involved in strange cults . . .

LIFE OF DREW CARSON

Sam Drew Carson was born in the North of Ireland and educated there at Wellington College and the Ulster Polytechnic. He completed his education in the USA at New Mexico Highlands University and the University of Arkansas and has traveled widely in North America, around the Atlantic and in Europe.

Drew worked as a seaman and fish-gutter in Vestmannaeyjar off the coast of Iceland. He lived and worked in the Irish and Western Isles Gaeltachts and was married in Welsh-speaking Carmarthen after which he honeymooned in Belfast.

He has told his stories, composed and sung his songs, seeking storylines in Bristol and the English Westcountry. Drew has also lived and written in Nashville, Tennessee, in the wooded hills of Mid-America and from the Appalachians to the Ozarks. This was the culture that gave rise to the now worldwide Scotch-Irish country music.

In the USA, he also worked beside the bayous of the French-speaking Cajuns in the South and among the Western Spanish-speaking Navajos, Apaches and Pueblos of the Sangre de Cristo Mountains in New Mexico.

Drew has sailed far into the seas of old Gaelic and Oriental legend. After many years searching for inspiration for story and music, the author is still traveling and writing.

BOOKS BY THE SAME AUTHOR

ZENISUB
Fun and Games in Businezz
ISBN: 978-0-9561435-2-5
GOOD FOR A LAUGH
Six Funny Playscripts for Amateurs
ISBN: 978-0-9561435-3-2
HOME WITH A GOOD COMPANION
Amateur Pantomime Scripts for a Merry Winter
ISBN: 978-0-9561435-4-9
CLASSIC EUROPEAN LYRICS
Translated from the Gaelic, the French and Spanish
ISBN: 978-0-9561435-6-3
COMMONWEALTH
An Introduction to Business Economics
ISBN: 978-0-9561435-7-0
WEREWOLF MURDERS
Detective Felix O'Neill in a Crime Adventure
ISBN: 978-0-9561435-9-4
ORIENTAL GOVERNESS
Detective Felix O'Neill in a Crime Adventure
ISBN: 978-1-908184-00-9
WALLWAVE THE YOUNG SEA WARRIOR
Adventures of War Queens and Battle Heroes
ISBN: 978-1-908184-03-0
WALLWAVE THE SEA PRINCE
Adventures of War Queens and Battle Heroes
ISBN: 978-1-908184-04-7
WALLWAVE THE SEA KING
Adventures of War Queens and Battle Heroes
ISBN: 978-1-908184-05-4
THAT SILVER SHORE
Easter Musical with Ten Songs
ISBN: 978-1-908184-06-1
THE OTHER SIDE
Halloween Masque of Demons and Delusions
ISBN: 978-1-908184-07-8

SEE YOU AROUND
Pantomime of Bygone Fun and Frolic
ISBN: 978-1-908184-08-5
CULT OF THE WIDOW VIDOVA
Detective Felix O'Neill in a Crime Adventure
ISBN: 978-1-908184-09-2
WHITE ZOMBIES OF NEW CASTILE
A Sci-Fi Adventure
ISBN: 978-1-908184-10-8
EASTER AND SPRINGTIME
Six Playscripts about New Life
ISBN: 978-1-908184-12-2
BRITANIA
WarQueen of the Seagulls
ISBN: 978-1-908184-13-9
IVORY TOWER COLLEGE
One-Act Play
ISBN: 978-1-908184-14-6

Cult of the Widow Vidova

Detective Felix O'Neill in a Crime Adventure

DREW CARSON

Legals

Published by S. A. Carson,
29 Northleaze, Long Ashton, Bristol BS41 9HS, UK
Publisher's email: verygoodreading@googlemail.com

ISBN: 978-1-908184-09-2

TABLE OF CONTENTS

Chapter 1
A Mystery to be Solved

One day as Dr. Arturo Garzon sat quietly in the Promenade study that he shared with his friend Felix O'Neill he glanced at O'Neill and observed a faraway look in his eye. Clearly the master detective saw things in the far distance of his mind that were unseen to his friend. They had no query, no plea for help, no challenge or mystery at hand and so Garzon was completely mystified by O'Neill's demeanor.

Most of their previous adventures together had been in response to some specific request for assistance but this was to be a case where they set out to explore a more general problem of a worldwide and recurring nature. This turned out to be a unique case about the beginnings of a cult.

Eventually O'Neill returned as it were to reality and remarked, "My dear Garzon, have you ever considered that people go missing and are never heard of again, at least in the land of the living. This even happens while they are engaged in the most ordinary, routine and everyday pursuits.

"To be sure, Garzon old chap, some of the missing are found dead of natural or unnatural causes."

His friend nodded in agreement.

"Some wish to escape from creditors or other unpleasantness and some even wish to escape from their loved ones which is a strange but true thought.

"No doubt many escape from enemies or the late-acting, unsuspicious arm of the law. Perhaps they flee in fear of future disclosures. Some elope and so forth."

"Yet at the end of the day, often literally so, there are many who disappear for no apparent reason. I have been thinking about this mystery for quite some time now. Why, I ask myself dear friend, is this happening. Why?"

After sitting quietly and listening to Felix's reasoning, his friend replied, "I have no idea. Do you know why, dear fellow?"

"Certainly not, Garzon, that's why I asked you the question but I have had some idle speculations on this for some time."

"Come to think of it, I've also been having some thoughts on this phenomenon of late," said Garzon. "Anyhow, go on and tell me what you have come up with."

It turns out that O'Neill had long studied the fate of lost travelers and the misty cults that seemed to attract them.

"These cults don't necessarily spring from greed but often begin somewhere in the dark world of treachery," he said.

"It may be that two or three persons robbed and wrecked by the wiles of the world come together so that they can lament the undependability and stupidity of business friends, family or partners. They realize that in order to even survive in this vicious world, people need others who are like-minded to support them.

"Some people are often not strong willed enough to survive in the face of competition from ruthless others. It may be that wisdom, education, religion, family ties and contacts, law and common decency even money may not be enough.

"They will die in the gutter with others unless they try something new."

"So what do you think is needed?" asked Garzon.

"I just don't know," replied O'Neill. "But many seem to think they need a system given over to themselves, one that binds them together with others in self-help.

"Sometimes a long forgotten book of rules from some distant cult is found and adopted and revived. A few converts are made. The result is that a circle or cult is called together, not necessarily for greed but purely in self-defense against the stupid destructiveness and the random instability of the people who come and go.

"Over the generations, a cult may build up some real power so that all those who succeed in business or politics seem to be members of some secret society or other."

Garzon listened intently to O'Neill's insight into this phenomenon.

"Some of their members often live unknown and unrecognized among the rest of humanity, while others live in outback communes in far places set apart. To leave some cults, one simply walks out the door. To get out of others, one must be carried. But they all have one thing in common, they are groups set aside from the rest of society. That is, they are groups that exist for the purpose of benefiting the members who must help each other. Usually this is more a matter of lower orders helping the higher but always a smidgen of help trickles down or across to make sure the group survives."

It may have been thoughts along these lines that troubled O'Neill as he and his friend later investigated a cult that came to be recognized as the Cult of the Widow Vidova. For it was in the very region that they eventually decided to visit that an old widow was known to frequent graveyards in order to introduce mourners to her commune.

"I have been thinking of visiting a region called the Greenwood Hills where many have gone strangely missing and it may be that I can try to discover their fate as perhaps typical," said O'Neill suddenly. "Would you like to accompany me, old chap?"

"Of course Felix, dear fellow" replied his friend.

"We'll have to go and at least try to find out what happens to us. Right?"

"Yes, I suppose so O'Neill," replied Garzon with some but not overwhelming enthusiasm.

"But O'Neill, we must go well armed. We need to be wise if we are to survive. There must be dark forces lurking out there in the criminal wilderness of this world. Surely you must agree?"

"Exactly, old boy. We'll take guns and take care. Capital idea, Garzon. We'll start as soon as we can get things organized."

So began one of the most dangerous adventures, not from any individual appeal for assistance but from a whimsical stray thought – a mere idea that began to dominate the mind of the world's most innovative and dedicated master detective, Felix O'Neill.

The story tells of the little-known expedition on the part of Felix O'Neill and Dr. Garzon as they set out to explore the mystery behind the rumors of strange disappearances of innocent persons.

This story is told to illustrate a point which is universal with moral, practical and spiritual aspects and as a warning to the unwary.

These events could have happened almost anywhere, the place is irrelevant. It is enough that it all happened to Felix O'Neill and his friend Dr. Garzon, barely escaping with their lives. I sincerely hope that this tale will be a warning to many.

***

Chapter 2
A Mysterious Widow

It happened in a strange and gloomy place as the sun wore widow's weeds that swirled around in many shades of gray along a moody sky.

Few birds lived in the old graveyard but six blackbirds flew sharply upward to avoid getting too close to a scarecrow in a nearby field. The scarecrow grinned as he swung back and forth like a pendulum suspended from a nail driven through his throat into an old upright stick. The scarecrow made many shudder besides the birds as he measured out the passing hours like an old wag-at-the-wall clock.

For who is not afraid of the passage of time?

Indeed, it is strange how birds seem to desert a graveyard for no apparent reason. The dead lying there are supposed to be resting in peace and not influencing the living surroundings.

Do the birds know something that we humans do not?

In any case, in this old graveyard, there were few birds but the good news was that there were one or two sacrilegiously happy pups playing and jumping around. There were also a few beautiful horses here and there in ones and twos and fours drawing the carriages of the departed and their mourners.

An old woman standing at one of the gravesides seemed to be muttering and weeping to herself in apparent confusion with incoherent ramblings.

"Cults rule the world. All who would survive must join a circle. Fifty years ago I was an old woman. Resurrect the helpful dead. Our fourscore years and ten cheats us out of 50 years. Humans should live to be one hundred and twenty. The great circles get the army and police to kill for them. We must do our own policework if we are to live out our full timely lifespan. We must join together with our animal friends and refuse death."

As the woman in black tended the somber gravesite, few of the lingering mourners and visitors even noticed the apparently half-crazed old woman. But those who did hear her insane mutterings shook their heads in pity as they went on their way – except for two figures in the shadows who watched and listened.

Nearby, at a newer grave piled high with moist brown soil, a delicate girl hid herself. She was the frightened younger sister of a young widow. And from behind her elder sister's thick widow's weeds she stared in fear as her sharp ears picked up some of the strange old lady's murmurings. Meanwhile her widowed sister sobbed silently as she wept for the loss of her husband - so near and yet so far away.

Maria Voss was tall and strongly built with long red hair and a ruddy face. Her neck was set at a slight angle to her shoulders.

Her young sister Veretta was short, thin, weasily faced and wiry. Her hair was a mix of black and red, a sort of dark brown auburn. More pale skinned than her elder sister, she nevertheless freckled and burned easily like the rest of her ruddy family.

Maria Voss was mature for her years. She was a rather resigned young woman who had been born into pitiless poverty. However, she had gone to work as a young girl, cheerfully grooming horses which she loved and admired. She had been married to another young groom. They had worked happily enough in the stables of a roadside inn until her husband was thrown by his favorite horse, scared by a bolt of lightning.

While she and her young sister mourned over the grave of her dear departed husband, the sky began to cloud over suddenly, surely just a little too early for twilight.

The mysterious old widow at the nearby graveside was thin, broken and shaking as she tried to clean up the grave before the storm broke. As she did so, the younger widow continued to sob nearby.

But was the old widow really mad or was she rehearsing some strange litany with some obscure meaning?

The near-twilight storm was now brooding and brewing across the great green hills. The older lady, in black veil and widow's weeds, stooped down to clear away the dead flowers from the grave. Then she looked up at the sky that hastened her late and liquid gardening as the raindrops began to drizzle down.

Soon she hurried away as the splashes led to faster dashes and then a few splits of lightning followed by periodic smacks of weak thunder.

The younger woman and her sister caught the old widow's eye as they all hurried out of the graveyard.

It was clear that the two sisters, Maria the elder and Veretta the younger, were mourners from a recent funeral.

Two figures watched and listened from the shadows as the ancient crone cried out, "Come young ladies, you can both shelter in my carriage over there."

The young widow nodded gratefully. The sky began to darken and brighten alternately. Was it just dusk and a few threatening raindrops or was it a more deadly darkening and a slumbering storm? Who could tell when false storms so often brewed up in the hills and then died off in minutes?

Quickly, the young widow and her sister were ushered over to a large gray shabby carriage drawn by two angular black horses. The coachman that hunched over the whip with high hat pulled down to his ears and collar turned up, could have been asleep or dead.

Veretta became a little fearful and drew apart from him and the coach and spoke to her sister.

"Maria, is this another hearse with a coffin? If it is a hearse I don't want to go inside."

The young girl whispered, "Please don't make me go in there Maria."

Maria smiled an apology to the older woman then turned to her young sister.

"Don't be silly, Veretta. This is no hearse. This is just a riding carriage. It'll keep us nice and dry from the storm and, perhaps," she glanced at the older woman, "save us a long walk back to the village."

"Yes, of course," replied the old lady, "we'll be glad to get you both home safe and dry. We widows and poor people, even if some of us have a little more than others, should share what little we have."

Then, as the young woman and her sister took their seats in the carriage, the old lady continued, "Sad to say, there are so many in this world who are only out to help themselves and their own loved ones. As for the rest of us, we must scramble for the leavings as best we can."

The carriage drove away into the gathering storm and the older widow drew her high collar around her neck as she sat opposite the young widow and her sister.

"I am the widow Vidova. Perhaps you are not a widow? Just because I am a widow I should not assume that you are also one."

As the younger widow began to speak, the older woman held up her hand.

"What I mean is, it is clear you are bereaved. You have lost a loved one - a father, a husband, a mother. It is all the same when you suffer a great loss as I did just a few short years ago. We are the bereaved that is why we should try to help each other in any way we can. Life is short, too short alas." She smiled.

"That's all true ma'am but it was my husband who died just three days ago. This is our first visit since the . . the . . funeral. I am Maria Voss. This is Veretta Schmitt my young sister."

As the young widow spoke, raindrops began to splash against the windows of the carriage but not strongly enough to obscure the view of a magnificent four-drawn coach speeding past them. The four white horses were bridled in gold braid. Gold and silver trimmings and a coat of arms shone on the sparkling coach. The occupants of the great coach barely spared a downward glance at the passengers in the old widow's shabby two-drawn.

The widow Vidova waved her hand at the other coach and smiled again.

"That's what I mean when I say that most of the great ones do not care or spare a mere glance for the rest of humanity. You see I have made a lifetime's study of survival.

"Indeed, normal families invariably squabble with each other and this tends to bring them into disrepute and failure and sometimes even bankruptcy or jail.

"You see my dear Maria, in a few minutes when I leave you off at your village here I may never see you again. So I must get to my point now to discover if it is of any interest to you. Perhaps you have a good pension and no concerns."

Maria shook her head and sobbed. "No, we have no means of earning a living. We are virtually penniless."

The widow Vidova sympathized with Maria then she continued to explain to her about circles.

"Well, there are hidden circles in this great world. Who are they? What do they do that could affect you or me? Perhaps they can do more than you suspect, more than you fear in your most violent nightmares. Let me tell you, cults rule the world. Of course, they do not use the term 'cult' of themselves. They are the gray shadows behind all men of power. They are the secret establishments that cause rulers to do inexplicable things such as blackmail and bribes."

Maria and Veretta listened intently to the older woman.

"Beware of the self-help groups that help only themselves. There are only so many good things in the world and, unfortunately, we cannot all have the things we need. But they, they get what they want because they cooperate with each other. And yet, there are so many poor folks who pull and push, exclude, steal or stab each other. That is why the outsiders are weak but the insiders are strong. That is why the circle members are high up in their carriages while the others are down low on their knees.

"The circle members hold ceremonies, pin medals on themselves, parade in pomp through their mansions and palaces while others grovel and hide in the dark and dangerous places of the earth. It is these groups who rule along the sunlit rivers while the poor stand with shaky feet on the smelly ditch sides of disaster, poverty, ruin, idleness, disease and death. So the poor must find a way to help themselves just as the powerful have found ways to help themselves."

Maria looked deeply troubled at these words. "Well, the way of life is - you help others and they pay you for your work. The problem is that I don't know anyone who needs help."

The lean wrinkled face of the old widow smiled at her companions with surprisingly red lips and white teeth, displaying kindliness and relief.

"Well perhaps I can put you in touch with some friends of mine. We are a small self-help group who may be able to help you – that is, if you have no other plans."

The young widow relaxed and nodded hopefully, "I need to plan out our lives without my dear husband so I'll consider any good idea for myself and my sister."

But young Veretta, separated by so many decades from the old lady, continued to frown and stare fearfully at the shriveled hands and face of the wizened crone.

Unperturbed or perhaps unnoticing, the old lady continued.

"Poor people need their own self-help group or commune or whatever you want to call it. If not, they will surely find themselves pushed aside and passed by on the road. They will be left with only the scraps thrown away by the great circles.

The poor folks need to be selflessly dedicated to their cause if they are to achieve good land, food and security for a long and healthy life. If you don't have money, these things cost time and work."

Maria nodded sadly, fascinated by the plain truth of the widow's arguments. "Well, lady Vidova, what is work and time? I've worked hard every waking moment of my life and I've nothing to show for it - no home, no savings and little furniture – nothing, only a room beside the stables in the village inn for my long hours of cleaning, scrubbing and tending horses. So what good are work and time and dedication and trying?"

"That is my point Maria. Your work and time and effort are no good when the great self-help societies of this world have kept everything for themselves. You just cannot make it on your own."

Maria nodded in agreement.

"You will need friends and sisters in the struggle. In the same way, men need brothers to help them break loose from the chains of the great self-help clubs. These clubs set up their own hierarchies that are based on their family's position or power."

Fearfully, Veretta suddenly took hold of her sister's hand.

"Maria, you know that we have always been believers and members of the church. Surely God will help us?"

"Yes dear, I did say that God is good. He will help us but when and how? He uses people to do his will. Perhaps this wise and experienced lady will show us how."

The older widow shrugged and spread out her hands helplessly.

"I don't claim to be doing the will of God. Long ago I stopped trying to find out what that will was and finally gave up all efforts to understand," said the widow Vidova as she continued her tirade. "Yes, God is good and will no doubt make all things right in the end - in the next world. But my question is, Can we wait until then? Till after we are dead? For me the answer is - no. For you perhaps – yes. It's up to you. As for me, I must try to help myself and others now - not in the next world."

Maria nodded, "I see what you mean. I hope that my young sister here has a long time to go before she reaches the next world. Until then, I must try to help her gain life, health, safety and usefulness."

The older widow leaned back in her carriage seat and sighed as one who had completed a difficult task.

"Yes Maria. I'm so glad that I spoke to you. I know that you will be grateful that you found us."

Then she smiled serenely, sharpening and accentuating all her wrinkles.

"Look - just as you are an older sister to Veretta, let me be an elder sister to you. Sisters are family and families need to help each other. If not, we will surely fail and destroy ourselves and the big families will get all that belongs to us."

"Lady Vidova, does your group have a name?" asked Maria.

"Well, naturally, the great religious societies and families try very hard to destroy us. They call us a cult so that they can denounce, isolate and persecute us. Then they share out the world's riches among themselves. In that way they will have no competition for the gold or land or the souls, bodies and minds of men.

"So the result is that we have had to hide ourselves away in the remote places of the earth and change our appearances and names. We need to move across distances disguised as migrants or visitors. There are little known ways to regain health and live longer. That's why we love the great Greenwood Hills - so wild, remote and unknown."

"Lady Vidova, do the great religions and families and groups of men really pursue your little group and try to destroy you when you are so small and weak?" asked Maria.

The old lady laughed a thin and sad laugh. "The greedy of this earth do not like competition. They themselves started out small many centuries ago. Even at this moment across these hills members of ancient and noble professions are trying to track down our little group in order to destroy it.

"They have recognized that we have something good and different to offer to the poor folks. We offer something other than miserable handouts and they hate us for it. They are determined to keep the poor to use as cheap labor and also to locate us and root us out of all these beautiful hills."

As the widow continued talking to her two new companions, the carriage sped swiftly towards the village inn. Thunder began to snap and the sky-lightning began to blink across the sky.

The old widow relaxed in the carriage and looked at the two young women through slanted eyes. She was easy and pleased yet sharp and cautious - the way a cat slinking out of the bush looks at a group of birds quietly picking and pecking in the sun.

*

It was dusk and two figures watched and listened from the shadows.

After a memorial service was ended at the Episcopal Church, the worshippers filed out through the small graveyard surrounding the church.

An older man, leaning on a walking cane, stood beside one of the gravestones. He was tall and gray and his large ancient frame shook with grief.

The rector and deacon approached the man and noticed that he was weeping. Not wishing to be intrusive, the rector placed an arm around his shoulder, pressed tight and addressed a few words of comfort.

"Colonel Barkley, if there is anything we can do or any advice . . or help . . you know we're close by."

The Colonel shook his head and the comforters faded away respectfully and discretely with bowed heads.

However, out of the dark shadow of an old heavy mulberry tree a small slight form moved slowly towards the Colonel and gave a soft coughing sound.

"I buried my late husband nearby just a few years ago. May I ask, sir, was . . is . . this your wife?"

"Yes, ma'am," came a broken reply.

"Yes," said the strange figure, "My own dear husband was a healtharian, you know - a brilliant doctor but he died at only 88 years of age."

"Ah, only 88, that is surely a great age," responded the Colonel. "Indeed, my concern is that I may never see it. My dear wife died at 78 and I am 79. My constant fear is that I will die soon myself. I am not weeping entirely for my wife though I would give anything to bring her back but I am also grieving for my own mortality.

"As the poet said, the bell rings out, not for my wife but for me and for all of us. I have seen too many times when a wife dies that her husband dies soon after or perhaps the husband first then soon after the wife. In this case is it grief that kills or loneliness? What does it matter, life must end and that is that."

The veiled lady pointed to the gates.

"My carriage is at the gateposts, sir. May I lean on your arm for I am about 20 years your senior and weak at times - only at times, mind you."

The old one seemed to give a sinister smile in the darkness.

"Certainly ma'am, I had no idea . . ."

"That I was so old? I am the widow Vidova - well known to some in the field of longevity."

"By all means let me . . ah . . escort you, dear lady."

The old man shook his head, "You mentioned longevity. I'm sorry to say that longevity, or the lack of it, is what disturbs me at the moment. First of all my dear companion of 40 years passes on and then I begin to fear that . . that my own lifespan is coming to an end. I admit my faith in the hereafter is weak and I certainly don't want to pass on just yet but, as I said, it seems that many husbands and wives die within a short time of each other."

"Yes Colonel but it is usually after a long period of life together. Ah, here is my carriage. Thank you for assisting me. If you need it, my coach is at your service."

"Thank you ma'am, but I have a trap right here."

"Well, if your horse can wait, let us drive around for a few minutes as I must tell you something about longevity that might interest you."

Colonel Barkley approached a small boy who was sitting on the graveyard wall.

"Keep an eye on my pony for a few minutes more and I'll be back shortly."

The young boy saluted keenly.

"Yes, sir, Colonel! Yes, sir."

The widow's coachman was a tall angular darkly suited man in high hat and high collar. His long thin arms cracked the whip and held the reins almost in slow motion, languidly and sleepily, as they drove slowly around the town square.

The Colonel stared unhappily in front of him as his hands shook. His upper body trembled and shuddered terribly. His left elbow resting on his knee, his hand held his forehead to stop the shuddering. His fingers pressed into his temples like iron clamps.

The widow tried to comfort him as she placed a hand on his shoulder.

"I can see that you are overcome with grief and fear of death. It happens to us all at times especially when it is the death of our loved ones.

"It happened to me on the death of my husband. He was a healtharian who postulated a three-phase life of three times forty years. Forty years of youth, forty years of maturity and forty years of seniority - the three phases of learning, experimentation and practice. But how many achieve this fulfillment of the 120 years of life? Almost none, but if even a few can do so, it should be possible for all. What is missing from the life of the vast majority of humans? What do you think?"

The Colonel faltered.

"I have no idea, ma'am. I only know that I loathe the death of my wife and fear that death is coming upon me before my time. I know this has happened to others. I dread death."

"Just so," continued the widow with sympathy, "but you must understand that so many couples following each other into death is because they share the same food and sleep and air and drink and work and worries and hopes and problems.

"In a word - their lifestyle is often very similar. If you want to live, Colonel, you need a new regime, a new life-force, a new dedication to survival and vigor, a new viva following the philosophies of Vidova."

The Colonel sat quietly as he carefully took in everything that she said.

"You might wish to consider joining our commune where everyone contributes their complete resources to the group. Just as in the early church.

"You cannot make the break too soon from your old premature death-bound lifestyle. You cannot act too soon to save yourself from soon-coming death. When my husband died, I formed a commune. Some call us a secret circle because we all believe alike. It is for all those who wish to change their way of life with new diets."

"Of course ma'am but I do have a fair amount of savings and a pension so I suppose I would need to turn that all over to the commune?"

"Yes, we have all done that. Though, of course, we would require no real work from you in return for this, just a few advisory duties and an occasional word of witness to outsiders.

"Yes, your money would be pooled but I have found that money does not buy everything that the elderly need. Perhaps millions would be enough but no ordinary amount of money comes close. Food and clothes and a roof and some old cures are not enough. I found out when I began to get old that I had to greatly improve my own diet.

"Also," she smiled, "I had to avoid any greedy relatives and legacy seekers."

"Well, I've had the same problem, lady Vidova but I know how to say - No. I'm an old soldier, you know."

The Colonel straightened his back.

"Yes," continued the widow, "but I was afraid they were going to have me put away for care. It's not enough to be strong in a case like that."

The Colonel became nervous at this comment and nodded uneasily.

"And what," she continued, "about the trashing we get from the masses and the attacks from their dogs and children and the sneering from the useless law, if we complain."

She glanced sideways at him like a fox.

"Then there's the persecutory onslaught of petty officials - petty in job and salary but huge in their tyranny and hatred."

"Yes, we've all had these worries as we grow older, lady Vidova."

"Yes, Colonel, but let me put it more positively instead of sounding negative. I have found that the hidden assets are the best - goodwill of our friends, neighbors, good contacts, trust, respect, reputation, a safe place to live. Only huge amounts of money could have bought me these if I had not joined together with others of like mind to form a cult of friendship and loyalty."

As Vidova continued to converse with Colonel Barkley in her carriage, his mind was blinded and bound by grief and fear but something of the clear logic of the lady Vidova's words seemed to creep through the mists and mysteries of her words and flashed a cool sensible message to his bereaved mind.

"What good to hold on to one's personal fortune only to die soon?" the widow asked once more.

"I don't understand all of what you say. My thoughts are seared with sorrow and sickness at the present time but I understand one thing," he said, "if I follow in my wife's footsteps and do the same things in the same way - I will follow her soon to the next world."

The widow nodded wearily, "That is about what it amounts to, Colonel."

Thoughtfully the Colonel nodded as he stepped down from the carriage and took up the reins in his own small trap. As the young boy saluted again in enthusiastic thanks for the few coins received, the Colonel slowly and thoughtfully drove off to his home.

The lady Vidova sat back in her seat and smiled to herself well satisfied with her newly bereaved acquaintance as her black-suited coachman took up the reins of her coach and drove off into the distance.

***

Chapter 3
Out of the Storm

Felix O'Neill and his friend Dr. Garzon spent time exchanging thoughts about the dangers of traveling alone as they continued on their way.

O'Neill remarked, "Traveling is one of the most dangerous occupations in the world, Garzon. I would further state that this is no exaggeration, no figure of speech - it is literally true, at least as far as all ordinary people are concerned."

Garzon knew that he was in for one of O'Neill's long tirades on the topic so he settled back and listened. What else could he do?

O'Neill continued with his analysis of the dangers of travel.

"Armies and explorers, prospectors and migrants all travel but how many never return? Of course, a few wealthy folk travel safely aided and abetted by the comforts and protections of money. But then, they're not traveling the way most plain and ordinary folk travel, in ones and twos or in the most dangerous state of all – poor and alone.

"The ordinary traveler leaves behind his accustomed climate and culture and friends and as a result he becomes sick or too hot or too cold or out of place or alone - a perfect recipe for impending trouble or even death.

"Worse, even than the possible full-dress rehearsal variety, is the final stage performance itself. Here, travel puts the perfect victim within easy reach of the perfect killer - the killer who has no known connection with the victim."

Garzon was shocked.

"Felix perhaps we should reconsider and think about going back home."

O'Neill laughed at his friend and continued his tirade about traveling alone.

"Travel is the mist that covers the trails in the long annals of annihilation. It will obscure the answer to questions such as: How many pilgrims have been slain in the lonely places of the earth? How many runaways never return?   How many of those who search for a new way of life and leave their old haunts to find fame and fortune afar off are never heard of again - widows making a new start, jilted brides or deserted grooms, the petty criminals on the run, fleeing husbands and wives, truant sons and daughters?

"How many of these have gone into the mists of time forever? How many just taking a short journey suddenly and mysteriously disappear? Even a brief trip to the graveyard can be dangerous and not for the obvious reason."

At this comment Garzon's throat became dry and so he reached for a bottle of water.

"Would you like a drink Felix?"

"No thanks, Garzon," replied O'Neill as he continued his friendly tirade.

"One day, healthy normal people are there and the very next day they have disappeared and forever.

"In this world, one of the basic human rights and one of the national ethics is the right to move on and to try for success in new fields. To try harder for better ways and days further down the road. There is no taking away this right and likewise there is no protection against the deadly fiends of travel except perhaps to stay home and rot, which I have no intention of doing at this time, old chap."

At this point Garzon changed his mind and enthusiastically agreed with O'Neill.

However, in an age before any great home comforts, back in the bad old days, staying at home was not a particularly attractive option for these two enquirers.

Both O'Neill and Garzon had differing professional interests in pursuing their quarry.

Felix O'Neill was a consulting master detective and as dedicated as a human bloodhound in the protection of everyman's freedom to travel without the fear of a mysterious disappearance or even murder.

Whether their interests would put either one in a position of defending themselves in some dangerous situation, was entirely an open question.

Eventually, O'Neill and his friend

Garzon arrived at a vast area known locally as the Greenwood Hills. They were able to buy suitable transportation in the form of two sturdy horses that were named Glory and Medallion. They also decided to take along a Labrador named Moro who was recommended as a good watchdog to warn them of dangers in the night. They loaded up with all the supplies they needed and continued on their way.

The solitary figures of O'Neill and Garzon rode among the huge old trees as the two friends plodded their way further into the Greenwood Hills. It was a tree-covered range of remote mountains that included rivers, caves, creeks, secret caverns and ancient tombs with places to lurk. These hills covered hundreds of square miles and were often visited by mists and rains and storms.

The happiest of the five travelers was Moro the old black Labrador, loping along with tongue hanging out like a drunkard's shirt tail. Now and again he would look up for the approval of the two horsemen with the simple message, See what a good dog am I. Glory and Medallion were proud and brave horses.

The two men would soon find out that a few tales of a hidden circle had drifted out of these remote hills, only a few mutterings from drifters and a few mysterious disappearances here and there but no specifics. Indeed, any questions that they asked of the locals along the way would be greeted with – no, we don't know who this cult is, mister. Where exactly is it located?

Yet, despite the scarcity of witnesses along these thin winding lanes and narrow carriageways, it seems that more folks strangely disappeared here than in the populous homes, sweaty offices and the toiling places of so-called civilization.

Along the way the men had to make several stops at some of the small towns for supplies of food for themselves and their faithful companions, Glory, Medallion and Moro.

It was at some of these towns that they were able to pick up gossip and rumors from the locals about strange disappearances in recent years near to the town of Dungowan.

One such story was about the sudden disappearance of a young couple who had gone camping. They were staying at a local boarding house in the town and all their possessions were still there waiting for their return but they had never come back.

Seemingly, this was only one of many such odd goings on in and around the Greenwood Hills and in particular the hills around Dungowan.

This was enough to encourage O'Neill and Garzon to head in that direction. So they made sure they had all the supplies they would need for the journey and went on their way.

The two friends were now headed into the hills surrounding the town of Dungowan. They had been told of rumors that a mysterious cult had a commune hidden somewhere deep in these hills.

The rumors could not be tied down to any specific people or location. But to both O'Neill and Garzon, the rumors of a secret cult were a matter of profound interest.

The cool, sharp breeze and the raindrops gathered force as the sky blackened and the gods of the hills growled and flashed their eyes.

O'Neill and Garzon decided to take shelter and guided their horses off the beaten path to rest them under a large brownstone bluff. Their faithful dog Moro the Labrador was the least happy of the five as he hung his head low in fear and gave a weak bark.

There are powers of evil and powers of good in the universe - one to help and heal and build, the other to torment and to prevent and to destroy.

As O'Neill reminded Garzon, "At times it seems that bad weather is one of the outward signs of an evil presence at work.

"Yes, seamen often tell of invariably bad weather when carrying a corpse on board ship. It is as though the soul of the dead clawed and knocked to set the body free to roam in the green mountains of the ocean."

"I've heard those tales about the sea, O'Neill," remarked Garzon.

"Those who tell tales of far-off lands, tell of evil storms that travel with the terrible apparently undead," continued O'Neill. "There were blasts of lightning that came with man's attempt to become god and recreate man. And, to be sure, at times it seems that bad weather is just plain old bad weather. Just like that."

"Nevertheless," added Garzon, "there are times and places when hidden forces of wickedness seem to hide behind the elemental hatreds of storm and hurricane, tornado and rain.

"It may remain impassive, silent and still. Then, in the quiet of the winter forest it will jump out on the unsuspecting traveler and tear him apart without either warning or orderly prior notice. Surely this is far, far worse than murder announcing its presence in advance."

Felix O'Neill and his friend Garzon were at least forewarned.

The far misted Greenwood Hills still glowed in streaks of pale sunlight over in the south towards Dungowan but most of the sky was still overcast as they led their horses out from the bluff to the top of the steep hill and scanned the hills and valleys. It looked like a green sea of waves, wet from the storms of the rain as bolts of lightning stabbed the forest afar.

"What do you think, O'Neill? Is the storm going or coming back?"

"Nobody is wise enough to know that my friend," replied O'Neill.

Garzon nodded in agreement.

O'Neill continued, "But speaking as a careful student of weather I'd guess there'll be no return of the storm right here for a little while. You know, it doesn't usually clear like that unless the whole sky is about to get bright."

Then he pointed toward a patch of dullish sunlight to the south.

"Look, its growing lighter so we should be able to make it to Springs Glen before nightfall."

Garzon nodded, "With luck."

"Of course, that's only my best guess," conceded O'Neill.

It was as though the demons of the Greenwoods were outraged at O'Neill's humble attempt at prediction. Even as he spoke, a huge blast of thunder almost split their minds in two. It was like the crack of doom as the sky completely blackened again. Thunder, sheet lightning, bolts of lightning and rain washed down the windows of heaven all around them.

O'Neill looked at his friend Garzon and shrugged in apology, "Told you so."

They calmed their horses, Glory and Medallion into the partial, if dangerous, shade of a mulberry tree while champing down the purple-black fruit that had fallen to the ground. Moro cowered, hiding his face in his paws.

This was the kind of thunder that shatters the nerves of heroes. It was heart-piercing and somehow deeply threatening. There are severe storms and merely bad storms but this storm was defiantly malevolent.

"We'll never make it to anywhere in this weather, Garzon. I'm not even sure where we are."

The severe rain tore into their faces and clothes.

"Felix, we'll have to find some kind of shelter soon. This weather is too much for us and the animals," said Garzon.

"I know, old chap, maybe we could find a farmhouse with a friendly barn," replied O'Neill.

Glory and Medallion shuddered and neighed as they moved uneasily. Moro covered his eyes as he pleaded for help from his all powerful masters.

The lightning flashed all around them. It was a dangerous situation but one faced many times by travelers in the Greenwood Hills. The sickening sound of grinding and crashing branches and tree trunks broke through the thunder as trees became wounded soldiers in the terrible civil war between former comrades, wind and forest.

O'Neill and Garzon were both well equipped physically with top coats, gloves and hats and waterproof wrapping for their boots. But these two traveling professional men were not mentally ready for this elemental horror in the middle of nowhere.

As they sheltered from the storm, they began to wonder what on earth had caused them to start such a journey in the first place.

"Garzon tell me why does a mere curiosity, a need to know, send us out to this forbidden wilderness?" asked O'Neill.

"Felix I believe it's in places like this that our knowledge is most needed," answered Garzon.

"True, but there must be other places besides this," said Felix, as his voice trailed away in surprise for suddenly at that moment a young boy on a pony appeared alongside of them.

"Here you are. Been looking for y'all since I first saw you at the waterhole. Reckoned you must be lost and strangers?"

His voice was querulous.

They nodded.

"Yeah I mean strangers in."

Then he stopped and gasped for air.

"Need of help and hospitality. My paw, Big Billy would be real pleased to offer, to offer you a shelter for the night. Of course, the real head of the family is our old grandmaw who's very kindly."

His speech was troubled in part by the stoppage and in part by a singsong monotony. It seemed as though he had learned the speech by heart, badly.

"Follow me," he said.

O'Neill and Garzon looked at each other and shook their heads in relief. It looked as though the boy was just a little odd, not quite backward. But any port in a storm, they thought.

"Let's go Felix."

"O.K. Garzon."

"Our name's Driew," said the boy. "We's mostly Billies y'know."

"Billies?" asked Garzon.

"Sure. I'm Billy, Billy Boy. My paw's Big Billy and my grandpaw's Old Billy. Then we's two cousins Billy as well."

Garzon nodded, "It's nice to have family traditions Billy Boy."

"Yes, sir. See, folks is got to know who is which Billy so I'm Billy Boy. Get it?"

"Sure, Billy Boy, nice to meet you, I'm Felix O'Neill and this is Dr. Garzon."

"Are you a real doctor?" he asked.

"Yea, that's his profession – he's both a healtharian and a homeopath," replied O'Neill.

"My dad's bald. Can you heal baldness sir?"

"I'm a physician not a magician," quipped Garzon.

Billy Boy doubled over laughing.

Obviously an impressionable, easily amused young fellah, thought Garzon, who was not in the least upset by Billy Boy's attempt to make humor of his profession.

"Actually I'm Arturo. My full name is Arturo Garzon. People tend to trust you if you're an Arturo but not so much if you're an unknown stranger traveling in the wilds. So that's why we're introducing ourselves," lapsing into the vernacular, "Get it, Billy Boy?"

Garzon turned to O'Neill, "Tell me Felix," he asked whimsically, "why would a normally intelligent person with the rain pouring down his face try to philosophize?"

"Defiance of the elements perhaps," suggested O'Neill.

"Hee, hee, hee," chortled Billy Boy.

"We's real old, old-fashioned family folks. You'll feel right to home with US."

He emphasized the last word.

"Tho we's no ways fancy. We's just plain family. See what I mean? Family. See?"

Billy Boy's spluttering seemed to be for the purpose of reassuring the travelers that they would feel at home with Billy

Boy's relatives.

O'Neill nodded.

"Sure Billy Boy, we expect to feel right at home with your folks."

Billy Boy spluttered and nodded and grinned massively. "Yessir y'all. Yessir."

As he grinned, his teeth looked like huge pig-eating carnivores.

O'Neill wondered why the word family seemed to mean good. Surely that implied that single, unmarried, on your own, meant bad or evil. Hmm, weren't families only as good or bad as the individuals involved?

Billy Boy looked like a teenager. He grinned a lot and smelt of the pig-sty - not good but a healthy honest, farming smell. His eyes were dark blue and flitted from side to side as he grinned.

Billy Boy bobbed and ducked as he spoke, as though he were avoiding an invisible swipe of the fist. Perhaps this was a trait picked up in childhood as he ducked out of the way of other-Billy swings of the hand.

But if so, Billy Boy had outgrown the original fear, for his ducking, weaving about and head-bobbing were invariably accompanied by watery, teeth-dribbling exhibitions of tooth displays that would have done justice to a dentist's favorite child. His teeth were fairly white and clean.

Billy Boy's clothing was quite clean too and, for a backwoods boy, it was surprisingly new and of good quality. Clearly the clothing had been bought in expensive clothing stores, yet, oddly none of it matched. Long blue overcoat - city style, wide country hat, pink pantaloons, black Wellingtons.

No sign of a gun.

Billy Boy added with the self-pleased air of one expecting an accolade, "We's family folks, we is."

Billy beckoned and bowed continually to the two travelers.

"Yes, sirs, you'll like my family a whole bunch."

As the group went on their way, Moro the dog was more cautious than the others and so he slunk even lower and closer to O'Neill and Garzon.

***

Chapter 4
Poor but Hardworking Folk

It is a fact that the idea of the family is generally well thought of by social theorists. Yet many strange and scary and homicidal people have lived in families and those same family folks have been good to each other. But what if the family is loyal enough to harbor a criminal, loyal to each other but treacherous to others?

It is quite a stretch of the imagination for some people who rely on logic and common sense for many of their values to understand the common association of the term – family. Just how does the word "family" come to be synonymous with "good" or "decent" or even "law-abiding?" Such is the logic of sentimentality - families are good and help themselves therefore they must be kind to others also.

Some of these thoughts may have

occurred to O'Neill and Garzon as they were screeched at by the wicked witch of the sky.

They followed behind Billy Boy with their two drenched horses and one wretched dog. The group shivered as Billy Boy led them to his family farmhouse.

However, neither O'Neill nor Garzon admitted out loud their doubts about familyism, as hope of a dry, warm, safe refuge overcame experience of the world as indeed hope usually does.

Billy Boy's home was fairly close by but well hidden away from the regular trail. They would never have found it but for the boy. The house was a squarish, two-story, wood-built farmhouse sitting in an isolated spot. Somehow it seemed sinister and crooked as the back of the house leaned against a sheer cliff face that glared down bleakly upon the small farm. There weren't many outbuildings, perhaps enough for some pigs, poultry and a pony or two. But this was not a place for any big rancher.

"Good work, Billy Boy," said his father as he came out, followed by several hill folk, to greet the strangers.

Big Billy patted his son on the back like an obedient retriever.

Then, bowing to the travelers, "Hee, hee, hee, y'alls wet as a spaniel's whiskers. Wasn't this nice of the boy? Good boy, Billy Boy. Welcome to our poor home, folks. Come on on in out of this here rain," as he ushered O'Neill and Garzon into the house.

Big Billy was jolly and happy and backslapping. He was double-chinned with a long snout of a nose, unshaven, pot bellied and somehow managed to be both obsequious and menacing at the same time.

Still, he greeted the strangers with a wide gaping display of bad teeth. He was almost groveling as he welcomed them.

"It's real nice to see y'all. Just make yourselves to home. Anything you need, just holler."

Big Billy was well named in other respects. He had a big belly and was clearly a big bully. His manner was to intimidate people by his size and the friendliness of his speech, then to play for laughs as one of the gang.

Some bullies are serious and scared underneath but Big Billy was a natural, an original and scared of nothing. His friends considered him to be as crafty as a centenarian fox, as fat and wobbly as a fairground wrestler and as smelly as a pig-sty in July.

As for wit, big fat Billy was as roly-poly funny as any music-hall fall guy. One could imagine him dressed in coat-tails, black bowtie, standing on the stage. Truly, Big Billy was a jolly soul, lost in these remote hills. He should have been in London or New York - on the stage, of course.

"And co-starring the funny man from Greenwood Hills - Big Billy Driew. How about a big hand for Big Billy?"

But he wasn't in any big city. Garzon and O'Neill had to consider how to react to him in these here hills, tonight.

Billy Boy cheerfully pointed to a small woman. "This here is my maw, Big Sister Willamena. I told you we was all mostly Billies."

A tiny woman with a miserable-looking expression on her face gave a nod. She was a sullen weasel with a sharp face that looked mostly at the floor.

It was clear that the Driews were a large clan but it was by no means clear right away who was who, due to the strong family resemblance in the shadowy light of the rambling farmhouse oil lamps.

Two thin-faced but healthy looking children were fighting and shouting in and around the covered porch as they ran around the feet of their parents. They were grabbing gold and silver buttons from each other as they argued and fought over who owned what.

The children seemed to be fascinated by the visitors and examined O'Neill and Garzon from head to toe with wide staring eyes. They stared and gaped as if they had never seen strangers before.

Big Billy grabbed the two children as though they were kittens. He held them by their loose clothing at the scruff of the neck and shook them around. They hung loose and limp in his hands and then became scared and suddenly silent.

Old Billy spoke softly to them, his

voice almost purring but laced with a harsh grating undertone of menace. "Say y'alls sorry to the fine gentlemen that have favored our lowly home with their kindly and much appreciated visit."

The kids hung limp, stupid and silent and scared and stared blankly.

"Oh that's all right kids," said Felix quickly, "you're only kids-a-playing. We ain't no ways put out, is we Garzon?"

"No suh," agreed Garzon with enthusiasm as he too lapsed into the vernacular. "We just love to see y'all so lively and friendly. Just reminds me of when I was a little'n myself. These are sure mighty nice kids, Billy."

Billy dropped the kids from his huge hands and grinned with pride at the compliment. The children ran off in silence and disappeared into the hollow burrows of the old farmhouse.

The Driews' sudden changes in mood were a little disquieting to the visitors but seeming to sense their unease the Driews renewed their groveling and pandering.

"Why, you fine folk does us proud to give us a chance to shelter y'all from the storm," said Big Billy.

However, Garzon remained briefly thoughtful about the children. Something reminded him of his own early life. Some kids seem to grow up in a continual state of warfare with each other. It's not always brothers, sometimes it's brothers and sisters or just sisters. It's hard to know how this happens in some cases and not in others.

Usually the parents take sides and intervene, ostensibly to secure "justice" or to redress an unfair situation or "stop the quarreling" but it's fairly clear to an outsider that the parental interference, usually to support a favorite son or daughter, only keeps the pot of trouble on the boil.

That's how it was with the two younger Driew boys. Tit for tat, don't do that to your little brother, let your big brother have his way for once. If I catch you doing that again to your brother I'll kill you and on and on and on.

It reminded Garzon of a dog pit where dogs were set to fight each other. The kids were being encouraged subtly and perhaps unconsciously to fight with each other by the fact of the grownups taking sides in the petty squabbles. There was something not a little disconcerting in this subtle child-baiting, masquerading as orderly peace-keeping.

"Why, you all po' folks mightabin killed out there. Just come right in here folks and make yourselves at home in our warm living hall. Let me take your coats. I see you all is travelers. You's as welcome as next of kin - or maybe I should say - next of kill. See, we's always fighting with our kinfolk."

Big Billy pointed a finger at his family and laughed out loud, "Ha, ha, ha, I'm Big Billy."

"I'm O'Neill - a detective. This is Dr. Garzon, a homeopath."

"Well this is a great honor for humble po' folks like us - poor but 'onest and hardworking, that's us — my goodness, a detective and a homeopath, why we's great believers in home remedies, we is."

"Homeopathy is not," began Garzon but realizing the pointlessness of a long-winded lecture, he added lamely, "not generally well understood or appreciated. I'm glad you all are great believers in it."

Around the room, Garzon could see nods of enthusiastic agreement from various family members.

"It's simple healthics for sure," he continued. "Just a matter of finding the right watered down remedies that will gently help the body to heal itself. I also practice some allopathic cures and surgery. But here in the outback there are few such opportunities so that berries, nettles and other herbal remedies seem to be the order of the day."

"Yes sir, Mr. Doctor." Big Billy helped to take in the saddle bags, handling them fondly but curiously. "Ah, yes, books. I like books. They're valuable you know."

Then several other members of the Driew clan who had been gaping open-mouthed at Garzon's brief and friendly speech now began to come closer and speak to the travelers.

The horses champed uneasily in the storm; Moro slunk into the shadows under the porch in the hope of becoming invisible.

Indeed, Moro the black Labrador slunk very low and wet and mournful, in the cold, biting rain. In this world there are only two kinds of dog, good dogs and bad dogs, nice dogs and mean dogs or was it sad dogs and lucky dogs.

Well anyhow, Moro seemed to be saying with his remorseful, please-help-me, I'm a good dog look, "Here I am being treated like a bad dog, whereas, as you know very well, I'm one of the kindest, friendliest, playfullest dogs in these here hills. This ain't fair."

Moro "belonged" to both O'Neill and Garzon, having been given to both of them as they made their way through a remote farming area. He was the nearest thing to family both of these single men had seen in a long time as tracking down missing persons in remote areas was a lonely job, strictly for singles.

Moro naturally assumed that rain and sun and storm, like food and water, was the result of human magic or some kind of manipulation. As demigods, O'Neill and Garzon were perhaps responsible for poor Moro's misery. Maybe if he whimpered and whined a little they would remember his good behavior in better weather and relent and somehow mitigate the waiting and the cold and the wet.

However, one of the clan spotted the uninvisible one and Moro was led off protesting to the barn, howling with self-pity and fear and dread of abandonment. Even the friendliest of farewells and see you in the morning old boy failed to reassure him. His head was hung low in an effort to prove what a good and compliant dog he really was. Moro's long lingering-backward looks, all notwithstanding, he was led off in abject mental agony by one of the Driew kids.

The Driews were firm, no dogs allowed in the farmstead. Also, as soon transpired, no guns and no strong drink neither.

When Garzon and O'Neill later got a chance to get alone for a few minutes, they related their observations about the Driews.

"I'm uneasy about this place Felix," muttered Garzon.

"Relax. Moro is not at home here and

I suspect that there are two others out there who are uneasy as well," said O'Neill.

"You mean Glory and Medallion? asked Garzon. "They're just fine - why they were noshing like . . ."

"No, they objected to coming here and so they should have and so should we," said O'Neill. "There's something wrong here and the horses are not at all settled. They were champing and nervous and so is Moro. Hear him howling and hear the horses whinnying!"

By now the two travelers were well inside the old farmhouse as they shook their hats free of rain and entered the main living area. Old shabby furniture ranged around the room, several doors led to anterooms and to the kitchens. A huge flight of stairs led to a balcony that surrounded and overlooked the great room. In fact this was a typical old fashioned farmhouse living area.

The smell of chickens, pigs, buckshot, dogs and dirty dogs all seemed to mix together with honest human sweat to make up a smell like a hillbilly punch. It was a real stink heaven. This smell was distinctive although the house was well cleaned and swept and aired by the Driew womenfolk but behind all these smells was the smell of something worse, rotten, something like the smell of sick dogs or was it the smell of something more sinister. It was faint, in the distance but it was there, however vaguely. Was it the smell of butchery of pigs? Not in the living quarters surely?

Old Billy, the grandfather, was a lean and wizened man with a cunning coyote of a face. Not a man to mess around with despite his age.

The grandmother of the pack had a face that was wrinkled and burrowed like old tripe. Her natural teeth were long gone but her mouth was filled with surprisingly white dentures.

O'Neill raised his eyebrows and pursued his lips as Garzon exchanged a glance of recognition at the sight of grandmaw Driew.

Some of the older folk had a strange sense of presence with intensity, a dynamism that immediately attracted attention, especially their black-robed grandmother.

The younger folk were all more peripheral, less demanding. It was as though they were livers of life in a lower key like Cousin Sam, grinning and nodding at the visitors, as obsequious as Big Billy but without his menacing aura.

Cousin Sam was continually washing his hands in the invisible soap that seemed to be the most plentiful commodity in the Driew homestead. He motioned to the visitors to shed their wet outer clothing and examined them with shrewd curiosity as though he was searching for something missing.

"What an honor to have educated folks, doctors and detectives in our humble old shack," cringed Sam's wife Sarah, her eyes floating around in deep sunken sockets, she managed to look immensely glad to see the strangers and yet scared out of her wits at one and the same time.

"If you want to shelter here from the storm there's something you ought to know."

"Yes?" asked Dr. Garzon.

Big Billy broke in obsequiously,

rubbing his hands.

"It's just that I'm sorry we'll have to ask you to leave your guns with Old Granny here for safekeeping. But do this later, of course, later, if you like our hospitality and want to stay the night. Later like, not now, gentlemen, just iffen you feel like it, if you stay like. See?"

"Sure, we don't tote any big guns, just a couple of small inside pocket equalizers." O'Neill tapped his waistcoat playfully. "We don't mind handing them over later on I mean - to Granny, do we Garzon?"

"No, indeed, no - not at all."

However, Garzon exchanged a few suspicious glances with O'Neill.

O'Neill tilted his eyebrows towards the storm which still raged threateningly then he muttered under his breath, "Six of one and half a dozen of the other, the storm or a strange household."

***

Chapter 5
A Happy Family Dinner

Garzon looked around the room to see if even one of the Driew clan was less strange, less freakish than the others.

His eyes rested on another cousin, later named as Clem who was a tall, black-mustached and handsome young man.

Clem, a little impassive and dull, was still nodding a courteous and pleasant welcome to the visitors. He seemed to be genuinely pleased to see the refugees from the storm as he extended his arms towards both of the travelers.

"Come right in folks and join our table. Have some of our hot food and drinks. We was just about to eat dinner over here."

Felix O'Neill took careful note of the tableware which seemed oddly out of place in a poor farmhouse in the middle of nowhere.

Clem continued with his invitation to join the group for dinner.

"Yes, I see y'all looking at some of our fine tableware. And, well yes, we's po folks but we work mighty hard and trust the Lord. Tho he hasn't given us much money, he put in our way - mostly by bequests - a few little home comforts. That the proof that we's good and right-living folks, you know.

"It says in the good book - The good will rejoice and prosper. So if providence has prospered us just even a little bit, that means he loves us."

Garzon interjected, "Well that's good to know that you're on the right track."

"Yes indeed. So I must say to y'all strangers here y'all can trust us to give you a real good night's rest and sleep. Don't worry about your bags and gear and horses they'll be well seen to and the ole dog and all. No offense to y'alls own religion - no charge neither."

O'Neill began to think things over and shrugged. What was going on here? Were these just harmless farming folk or an outpost of the Cult of Vidova about which they had heard some rumors? If the latter, he and Garzon were well prepared for such an eventuality and more than ready to step into the trap in order to trace any guilty parties.

O'Neill shuddered not only with the cold and exchanged a glance with Garzon that seemed to say, "Take care and take all with a pinch of salt."

As they all sat down over the huge dinner, the family helped themselves from the heaped communal plates on the central table and the two storm-hungry visitors, after an initial pause, followed suit as they took careful stock of the family.

"There, have some more cheesy sauce. Help yourselves to some more piked pig and a few more sawney beans."

Their names for white sauce, diced pork and pinto beans may have been a little idiosyncratic but the plates were appealing nevertheless.

It was as though the entire family flourished, not only in the faraway green hills but in a remote village of verbal isolation, living as a law of words unto themselves.

Big Billy, his mouth full of potato, tilted his head appreciatively at the two travelers and then raised his eyebrows cheerfully.

"Why, you fine folk does us proud to give us a chance to shelter y'all from the storm. It's a real privilege to help people. It makes us feel real happy to know we're doing some good in the world. That's what we're here for - to do good."

Big Billy's sister Doreen nodded in support of his little homily. She was fat and mostly vacant, intellectually a non person, yet strong and healthy.

But their guests noted her husband Jason was the most zombie-like of all the Driews. His eyes gazed far into the next world, seeing all and content with it, yet his slight smile was not of the mouth or even of the face, but of the eyes only.

"What a sinister fraternity," Garzon thought.

O'Neill asked himself, "Can we trust this creepy rabble?"

Suddenly Big Billy broke the silence

and began to apologize for his gluttony by referring to his imaginary old pal 'Slim' in the hope that this would put his two guests at ease.

"I bumped into one of my cousins the other day and you'll never guess what he said – Can I ask you something kind of almost personal Big Billy?"

"Certainly, Wilbur," I said.

"Have you heard from Slim recently?"

"Yes. I certainly have, Wilbur." I told him.

"Fact is, folks I can see him even right now from here in the shadows just outside this big dark window. There he goes . . ."

Big Billy pointed outside and gazed dimly into the shrubbery surrounding the farmhouse.

"You need to get back in touch with him Big Billy," said Wilbur. "After all, he's your old buddy, right?"

Again Big Billy peered through the window and said, "You're right about that, Wilbur, he certainly is that."

Then he waved to his imaginary former self, lurking outside.

"Hey, come here Slim.

"Look Slim - I'm on a new plan.

"No more greases or fries.

"No more white flour-based foods.

"No.

"Not another slice of bread ever or those great pies that Mother bakes. Sorry Mother. But I needs to keep Slim happy.

"Honest, old buddy I still wants to see you again, real soon.

"Now look Slim, you really must believe me this time - see we goes back a long time you and I does. Don't you remember we used to be such great pals. I really means it this time Slim, no strong drink, not even coffee - mild tea only, whole foods only - the healthics diet for sure.

"Whole cereals, like brown rice. See?

"Fish, fruit and veg only - hardly any milk, just a few nuts and seeds.

"Juices? Yeah, that's right Slim. Juices - fresh only, hardly any fermented except apple - no I meant only a very little - yes I understands you Slim.

"It's slim food only from now on. I'm turning over a new leaf. See - it's a dock leaf - and it's all I'm having for dinner.

"All right then, we goes back together to when we's were both like twins, thin as a slice of apple, so what's the matter, Slim? Why turn your back on me, old buddy? You can still be a friend, can't you?"

While Big Billy went on talking about his pal 'Slim', O'Neill and Garzon glanced at each other with raised eyebrows.

"My old buddy, if I did something you didn't like, I'm sorry. Honest, Slim, I'm real sorry. Hang in there, don't go Slim. Where are you, anyhow Slim? Slim? We're still pals, ain't we? That's what I like about you Slim, old buddy, always fooling around and all just like any other close friend. I'll soon catch up with you out there. No kidding now Slim? You'll see. Now, where has that waster, that ruffian, that blackguard of an old skinnymalink gone?

"Slim, still pals, right? Aren't we? Aren't we? Slim?"

At last, he seemed to lose sight of his old mate out there in the forest and garden shades. Probably never to catch up with him again.

"That's how I got left behind with this

gut. And that's why everybody calls me Big Billy. And I don't mind it at all cause that's what I is."

Then Big Billy patted his solid gut and shook his head sadly but continued to stuff himself with everything on the table.

At the same time, the others shoved each other enthusiastically and laughed and tittered at his confession which they had heard many times before.

At first, both the travelers had felt a little uncomfortable with these friendly but freakish country folk. Still, they were very grateful for the hospitality and good humor. A storm such as this could easily cut down men, horses and dog as easily as the trees.

But little by little O'Neill and Garzon began to change their minds about the Driews. Why be suspicious of such simple, generous folks and why question their kindness? True enough, people especially in these hard outposts are supposed to help each other. Is humanity so evil that one must try to unearth hidden, envious intentions as the underlying motivations for all kindness and hospitality?

The Driews were unlovely and ugly and odd and poor and uneducated but did that have to make them objects of suspicion? Indeed, the clan seemed more likely to be the victims of evil than its perpetrators.

One point of contention was suddenly addressed by Cousin Doreen, "My poor little brother got shot by accident when he was out a-squirrel hunting. Fell on his gun running down a hill after a squirrel. Guns are bad. If only the good folks would ban the gun."

"What about squirrel hunting, is that bad?" asked O'Neill.

"Nope, but I guess we could set traps if we put our minds to it," responded Big Billy. "See it's like this, we have no objections to a gun or two for hunting and self protection while things are rough and tumble but if folks would get to praying and get together and help other folks and not steal from each other's traps then maybe we could do without guns. See?"

"I don't see," responded O'Neill, "I don't see at all. I don't agree. Why we . . ."

"Just a minute Felix," broke in

Garzon. "We're guests here. It's not for us to offend."

"Oh, we's not offended," cried out Big Billy.

The rest of the clan heartily agreed with nods and nos as he went on to explain.

"It's just that we's religious folks and we don't hold with strong drink and guns and people not trusting each other."

His mouth was stuffed with pork as he splattered, "Ain't that so folks?"

"Yes sir, Big Billy, yes sir," agreed the rest of the clan.

"You see we's po' folks but we's got some standards. See what I'm saying?" went on Big Billy. "We don't hold with guns or strong drink or dogs in the house. Hee, hee, hee."

The whole Driew clan seemed to find this philosophy exceedingly witty and chortled gleefully to each other as Big Billy continued his tirade.

"Now we know that providence watches over all of us, so what do we need guns fur? See what I say? Or why would we need dogs to warn us when our good angel would do that for us? See what I'm saying? And why would we need strong drink to dull our wits when we got so little wit to begin with? See, what I'm saying? Haw, haw, haw - right Cousin Clem?"

"Right Big Billy," responded Clem.

Big Billy continued, "A few drinks and some of us would just plain stop thinking plum altogether. Right, grandpaw? Haw, haw."

Seeing that he had a big hit with this speech, Big Billy repeated, "No guns, booze or dogs here in this Christian home, no suh."

"Well," added O'Neill as a last resort, "it could be argued that every man has a right to self-defense but yet what is the best kind of self-defense against lies, duplicity, illusion or corruption. You need to divert the onslaught of these great destroyers of man from his fellow man. What you need is something better than a gun or a knife. You need something like a good witness, or perhaps a law book, maybe a true and fair record. We've no guns, have we Garzon?"

Garzon shook his head.

"You've no objection to our taking the bag of good books to bed with us?" O'Neill asked. "That one of our bags is all books. We'll give you all a copy of the good book as well if you like."

"Oh no sir, we have one of our own, thanks," responded Clem.

Suddenly Felix O'Neill stood up and handed his small handgun to grandmaw. Garzon did likewise.

Then both men opened up their book bag for inspection. The books were all respectfully and carefully handled but not opened by several of the clan. Then, seizing up the saddle bag with the books, O'Neill and Garzon followed Big Billy with his lamp up the shadowy stairs and into one of the bedrooms.

"I've had Big Sister leave these two candles for y'all to read. Have a good night gentlemen and iffen you need anything just holler."

Then the host backed off, bowing and nodding and grinning but still holding the oil lamp firmly in his huge fat hand.

O'Neill and Garzon made themselves comfortable and then when O'Neill was certain that his host had gone, he motioned to Garzon to sit down and the two men spent some time comparing thoughts on the evening's events before they retired for the night.

***

Chapter 6
The Intruders

The storm was still raging outside as O'Neill and Garzon crept coldly into the huge old farmhouse bed. But although the storm was less vigorous, less cold, it was more insidious now that they were within walls. Out in the open forest they had felt in more immediate danger. The storm was a demon clawing with sharp nails at their raw faces. Now it was more like the threats from a wicked old witch ranting and raving and shouting and cursing and screaming outside the fortress of her enemies.

"I'll get you for that," she screamed. "I'll put a spell, a curse on you and yours. You'll never prosper and your descendants will be servants of hell forever and you'll regret the way you treated me."

It seemed as though Moro the dog continued to howl a warning to its masters that there was danger nearby. The dog sensed it in the minds of the people around him and spelt it out quite clearly in wail after wail as he repeated the message continually – beware, be careful!

Why could they not understand?

All Moro knew was to keep repeating the message – beware, be careful! Only the physical limitations of throat, voicebox and wind could stop him as he continued to give howl after howl.

Back in the guestroom of the Driew farmhouse O'Neill and Garzon heard and almost understood. Not quite but almost. Despite their tiredness, both men could not sleep.

"Why is Moro going on like that?" asked Garzon. "He's never taken all that badly before to an overnight sleep in the doghouse? Sure he likes to be with us but why is he going insane tonight. It's not even a full moon."

"It's just the storm," O'Neill assured his friend, "just the storm, that's all."

Garzon shuddered as he recalled tales

of travelers missing in the Greenwood Hills - had they been victims of storms, floods or renegades? It's a bad land for travelers, especially those with valuable merchandise or so he had been told ominously.

Their room was dark, lit only by a faint moonlight and stars through the window as they lay down in the big old fashioned four-poster bed.

O'Neill asked his friend, "Why did you think they were so anxious to disarm us?"

"Why do you think, Felix?" responded Garzon. "I'm not even sure the latch on our bedroom door is safe."

"This is supposed to be hospitality here. It's not a hotel room where we can demand a locked door," responded O'Neill. "I'm afraid we'll have to take turns sleeping tonight, old chap."

"Yea, I see what you mean," conceded Garzon.

"Maybe it's no big deal," suggested O'Neill. "It could be that some of the kids are thieves and the others don't want us shooting them by mistake for serious intruders."

Outside their room was poorly lit.

Suddenly they heard a small voice speaking. It sounded sharp and hurt and even offended, "That ain't true mister."

Then another small voice spoke up.

"We ain't thieves. We wouldn't have stolen nothing. It's going to be all ours anyway."

"Yip," added the small voice, "when they puts you in the cave, everything in your bags will be paw's anyway and that means ours."

As O'Neill and Garzon's eyes got used to the poor light they quietly and inconspicuously took advantage of the darkness to rearrange the contents of their saddlebags. They filled them with enough pillows and blankets to make it appear that they were sleeping in the bed partly covered with blankets.

The first child spoke up again.

"They really are gonna put you in the cave like the others, aren't they?"

O'Neill's voice was a little shaky.

"Sure you bet you, kids. You bet that we're headed for the cave."

"Can I have your books mister? I can read a little. I promise to learn more," said a small voice from outside the room.

At this time, a faint sound was heard coming up the stairway.

"Quick, let's get outtah here," said one of the children's voices.

"No," said another.

"Come on you toad, we're not allowed in here."

"No. Ahh don't pull. You're hurting me. Please."

"Come on then."

"All right. I'm a-coming. There ain't no need to be . . ."

Then the two small figures departed as lively and swiftly as ghosts into some long hidden hole in the beamed ceiling.

"Are you feeling what I'm feeling?" asked O'Neill.

"It's not a cold shiver, is it?" replied Garzon.

"Yes it is and it's colder than the shivers I got during that thunderstorm," said O'Neill.

"There's no point in trying to make a break for it. They've probably locked up our horses."

O'Neill relit the remaining fragment

of candle and they continued to unpack their saddlebags. Their main interest lay hidden in four books which had been hollowed out some time past and where their main guns had been hidden.

The thought crossed their minds that perhaps the children had been playing a fantasy game. It seemed possible with the passing hours and it seemed even likely. But was it worth staking your life on?

Felix O'Neill and his friend Garzon with guns in hand took up crouching positions in each corner of the room alongside the head of the bed facing the door. This gave them a better view of anyone entering the room.

The saddlebags were sleeping peacefully in bed – hollowed-out books and all. A faint sound of sleeping, staccato breathing and light snoring floated out from the room, just loud enough for anyone listening closely at the door cracks to catch the merest hint of persons asleep.

Suddenly, two figures burst into the room - Old Billy and Big Billy. They were silhouetted clearly against a light in the corridor like shadows from another world.

The two figures loomed like ghosts of long dead cut-throats but yet not ghosts, truly alive with hatred and contempt for helpless humanity.

As the two Billys pumped their bullets into the sleeping saddlebags, Garzon and O'Neill fired back. There were at least four more of the clan in the corridor, guns in hand, all hell-bent on filling up hell.

When it came to killing there was no gender discrimination among the weird Driews. The women shot it out alongside the men and died alongside them too, in accordance with the old principle that says "those that live by the sword shall die by the sword."

As usual, the hell-fillers succeeded but this time only Driew clan members went to the bad place. Their old-fashioned pieces were no match for the rotary speed, weight and accuracy of the huge revolvers toted by their intended victims.

O'Neill and Garzon put down their guns and lifted their other guns also fully loaded before they crouched out into the darkened corridor.

Billy Boy made his last stand from a

shadowy corner.

A bullet sang past O'Neill's ear and for a split second he was disoriented and hesitated but Garzon was already filling the dark corner with a pilgrim for kingdom come. Billy Boy rolled down the stairs like a crow out of a tree.

Tallying up the cash register of the night's business, the score came to half a dozen dead, three seriously wounded and three missing.

It appears that while O'Neill and Garzon were disarming, trussing up and tying down the several survivors, the old grandmother had been able to make an escape with the infants by taking Glory and Medallion and poor Moro.

As O'Neill later explained to Garzon, Moro would have been unable to disguise their whereabouts if he had been allowed to remain with the horses. She had to escape and leave the clan's own horses in case some of them had been able to get away later. But this was not to be.

"Please don't kill us mister," cried out Old Billy.

"No chance Billy," responded Garzon.

"We'll leave that for someone who'll do a real good job on y'all - Hanging Judge Bailey Harkness at Dungowan."

A cunning look came into the eyes of Big Billy.

"But we ain't killed nobody," he said. "This was y'all's fault and no doubt just a little misunderstanding. Some of our kids went missing and we couldn't find them little critters nowheres."

He pretended to weep.

"We figured you had lured them into your bedroom. Now you know that ain't right. Naturally, we was red mad. In the confusion I dunno who started shooting first but I was trying to rescue our little boys and it was just self-defense on our part. We didn't mean y'all no harm. Why, you's our guests. Welcome as next of kin. Why don't we just bury our dead and forget it. Folk will believe our story because we's family and y'all is men traveling all alone. We won't bring no charges against each other. I'm sure our little boys would testify on our behalf if you really want to bring it to court. Let's just call it quits, mister, eh?"

Both O'Neill and Garzon looked at Big

Billy long and hard.

"Sure, we'll call it quits," said O'Neill, "when all of you are hanging out on the old judge's washing line. You see Big Billy, we know about the cave and those riddled saddlebags in the guest bedroom tell us the full story of what has happened before. It's no good lying any more, lying time is gone Billy. It's sleepy bye bye time, a long sleep for little old murdering folk like y'all."

Big Billy shut up and never spoke any sense again.

That night Moro had inadvertently achieved one thing - O'Neill and Garzon had felt a little uneasy, stayed awake and talked where otherwise they would have fallen asleep. In achieving that, Moro and his howls had saved their lives before he was possibly taken by the grandmaw.

If he had been left at the farm, it is highly likely that he would have leapt out of the barn bounding into the farmyard yelping like the pup he was at heart but this was not to be. O'Neill and his friend Dr. Garzon questioned high and low in the area for news of this faithful companion – man's best friend – but they never saw him again.

Death smells bad and it follows that a bad smell is the beginning of death.

After tying up and securing the prisoners, O'Neill and Garzon searched the house, armed with their heavy guns and kerosene lamps.

"Felix, over here," called out Garzon. "I think I've found it. This old pine dresser seems to be moving."

Garzon had uncovered a hidden door right at the back of the house. It was clear that the hideaway had been cleverly located to hide the entrance to a long damp cave. The old wooden-frame house was built under the shelter of a cliff overhang. The house looked as though it had been located underneath the cliff for safety and security, protection from storms, wind and sun. But the back of the house was hard against the entrance to a cave.

O'Neill and Garzon entered the cave, listening carefully in case any of the Driew clan had hidden themselves away. The entrance to the cave was several yards long and as they progressed, the stench of death and decay became stronger.

"It's unlikely that anyone is here," said O'Neill. "The grandmother and some of the children have escaped no doubt to far-off regions.   Moro has disappeared along with our horses."

"You can't be too careful. These guys are crazy," countered Garzon.

"Yea crazy but wily," agreed Felix. "This hideaway was planned and selected with real cunning. I'll bet there are at least ten dead bodies down here."

He was wrong again. Far into the wet and cold recesses they came upon a large high domed cave.   Inside the cave they found nearly two hundred skulls and the bones of unknown persons scattered around the sides of the cave. These were surrounded by old broken guns and plates and cups and water bottles and watches and dozens of other damaged items.

The Driews had evidently abandoned the old and broken items and left them to rot with their former owners - choosing only the best items for their own use or very occasional sale in far-off towns.

Some documents were later found showing that missing travelers for some thirty years back had ended up in the Driew museum. However, most of the bodies seemed to date from the previous few years when there had been more visitors to the Greenwood Hills. Quite a few old army uniforms were found rotting there - grim cadavers in a museum of wickedness - a morgue of madness.

The Driews had not taken sides between soldiers - all were grist to the mill. The yokels had dedicated themselves to their family business of missing persons.

The human body is just one big filth producing machine. How many hopeful spirits seeking out a new life in the great Greenwoods had their days ended here by the Driews homicidal hospitality.

It seemed to O'Neill and Garzon that the rows of decayed corpses sang out for justice and retribution.

In fact, there was a slight humming wind in the great dome blowing from remote crevices as the storm outside abated.

"You know Garzon when we hand these yokels over to Judge Harkness, along with their spoils of crime, he'll string them up within weeks," commented O'Neill. "They know this only too well so they'll never talk, never put us on the track of the others."

"Exactly," agreed Garzon. "Maybe we shouldn't hand them over and do a deal with them?"

"No, Garzon. I know how you feel. I understand your abhorrence of hanging but it wouldn't work. We'd be accessories to their next crime and remember they did try to kill us last night. These madmen and freaks are no healthics students. And how would we explain away the ones we killed in self-defense if we don't report their attack. Garzon, these hillbillies would have the two of us strung up if we gave them half a chance. I think our best hope is to persuade Judge Harkness to give them life instead."

Garzon nodded but with some doubts in his eyes and continued.

"Judges are supposed to have some concern for stopping future crimes. We could always try a mercy for information deal with him. He doesn't hang everyone, you know."

"I know," said O'Neill grimly. "I hear that his mother is still alive but other than that, from what I've heard, these are lawless hideaway hills. A judge has to be a hard man."

By now O'Neill and Garzon were back in the sunlight in the yard outside of the farmhouse.

The prisoners were silent but looking all around as though expecting a rescue from the depths of the woods.

Some of the birdcalls sounded strangely human and shadowy human figures seem to follow the procession but only a few and more as observers than rescuers. No assault was made on the sullen column.

As they drove the prisoners out into the forest, there was a heavy moistness and a smelly herbal dampness in the air that clung to the clothes and skin. Like a kind of filter that refined the true odors of the woods. It was the smell of after-storm. Broken trees, crushed leaves, sliding mud and flowers gone and small creatures dead all squeezed through a mist of rainbow and dewdrops.

All the birds of the forest were busy chattering to each other about their experiences in the storm.

"Well poor thing, she was nesting on the bough that fell. They flew off but the chicks were lost."

"They were too old to have chicks."

"You mean twas too late in the year."

"The tree fell on top of those thieving squirrels, it was providence."

And so on and on.

Neither the captors nor the captives understood a word but all understood the general drift - the storm was over and it was bird-talking time again once more.

Suddenly a massive, grizzled dog leapt out of the bush, planted itself stolidly at the roadside and seemed to roar in human language, "We'll get you and hang you high if you don't back off and free the prisoners now."

The talking dog retreated as O'Neill drew his gun.

"Did you see that?" he said to Garzon.

"Don't worry, I heard it too. That was just the Driew's ventriloquism."

Still, the two men felt uneasy until

they eventually delivered their captives into the safekeeping of the authorities in Dungowan.

***

Chapter 7
Back in Dungowan

Felix O'Neill and his friend Garzon duly delivered the surviving Driews to Dungowan where no prisoner had ever escaped from the jailer George Malmeurte and many were sent on the longest journey by Hanging Judge Bailey Harkness.

The Driews had seen to it that many travelers never reached their destination. Now Judge Harkness would see to it that they reached theirs.

When the Driew clan, bound together and under armed guard, had trudged sullenly into town, the populace had seemed to sense a coming hanging. Heads held as low as these could not belong to common or ordinary criminals. The dull hopelessness in the eyes of the captives as they stared ahead was the final proof of a soon-coming day of atonement.

Small groups of silent citizens had formed to watch the dread procession. Fear and joy stunned them. Anxiety fought with anticipation in the hearts of the onlookers as they struggled with the thought that such a fate might also be their destiny one day.

As Garzon remarked to his friend, "They're probably thinking, there but for the grace of God go I.'

"Maybe so," said O'Neill, "and I rather suspect that some of the businessmen are hoping that the sight of a few good hangings will bring visitors and money into the town."

"And the local church folk are hoping for some repentance as well. Who knows?" added Garzon.

In and around the saloons of Fortress Avenue, Malmeurte's deputies talked of the Driews screaming and yelling for mercy and acting crazy. They found it spooky and sickening even though they had been hardened by long service on death row. Yet official sources, Malmeurte and Judge

Harkness - even the local politicians - never talked too much about the case or gave out news on it.

Of course, it was all a matter of public record but no one wanted to publicize it too much. The sheer extent of the horror apparently taking place over a period of some 30 years stood as a kind of local embarrassment to law and order.

Perhaps they feared that visitors would be discouraged from coming and bringing money to those parts. Perhaps they were wary of criticism of their own ability or perhaps they were just too sickened and shocked to say much. At any rate, the case has rarely been written up.

Over a few drinks in the Cattlemen's Saloon on Fortress Avenue, O'Neill and Garzon talked to a group of subdued listeners about the case. Questions were shot at them as from a Gatling gun.

"How did you get on their track?"

"How did you find out about the Driew clan?"

"It was just rumors about missing travelers," replied O'Neill. "It's easy to get away with murder if no one knows that you've any connection with the victims. But over a period of years the trails of several missing persons pointed to this part of the country where not many people lived. We decided to set out to investigate and as fate would have it, we bumped into Billy Boy on the trail."

One of the locals remarked, "That was unlucky for the Driews."

The others all nodded in agreement and shook their heads in amazement.

"Apparently, they'd even married with close family members to keep the secret from outsiders," Garzon pointed out. "It was a real family business."

"The Driews had clearly figured they could better their lot by joining a remote self-help circle," said O'Neill, "but the question remains, how many other such cults are there in existence elsewhere in the world?"

Somebody asked, "How long have they been in business?"

"I think the Driews escaped detection for something like 30 years," so agreed Felix and Garzon as they talked to many in Dungowan.

"Everything they did was calculated with supreme cunning. The 'help us to get healthy' stance was calculated to disarm us and make us less suspicious. Right?" said O'Neill.

"Right," agreed Garzon.

"Our dog was put out so that he couldn't waken us when they were about to attack," Felix reminded his friend, "though he still did his best to keep us awake all night out of general concern for our safety."

"One thing I don't understand is, why did we find that wide variety of homemade booze back in their farmhouse?" queried Garzon. "Why did they pretend to be t-t? Was this just part of their self-whitewash to disarm us?"

O'Neill considered for a minute, "I think that was all part of their holier-than-thou plan to get the guns from us just like the rest of the religious-folks line of patter."

"They could have drugged the drink or the food?" suggested Garzon.

"I'm not so sure about that," replied O'Neill. "Communal plates and communal pitchers are widely used in these parts."

Some of the listeners butted in, "Yes, that's right mister. We sure do."

"Fancy separate bottles or set plates might have aroused our suspicions," continued O'Neill. "No, I think that everything they did and said was calculated to achieve as easily and certainly as possible the one simple act - murder. That's about it, those freakos were experts."

*

In the days of the hanging judge, Dungowan was a rough and nasty town. This was not to suggest that most of the folks in Dungowan were rough and nasty, not at all. It was only that the Rough and Nasty Gang seemed to predominate and set the tone for the town in general.

Dungowan was pitched on the border between plainsmen cattle folks and the hill farmers. There are bound be to a few rough edges in that kind of divide. No one blamed the town or the good folks in it but it was just not a nice place for refined retirement.

The true spirit of Dungowan was not

lawlessness - far from it. The true spirit of Dungowan was typified by a man who was the law itself – one of the most cold, logical, legalistic persons ever to wield real power – Hanging Judge Bailey Harkness. Death in the world, this was the true spirit of law and order.

Both O'Neill and Garzon watched the hangman as he lovingly fixed his ropes and pulleys.

O'Neill remarked to his friend, "You know Garzon, some men are driven by creativity or revolution or writing or arts or building or business or womanizing. All are creators. Others are motivated by money - a flexible currency. These are the renaissance men. Money can be turned into everything else at the flick of two wrists."

"Some people, even women, are motivated by power," added Garzon, "those are the problem persons.

"Power seems to be the motivating drive behind Malmeurte - the desire to dominate others. To make others subject to his will. To make people do what he tells them to do."

"Often enough, this was to stand still while he killed them," concluded O'Neill.

Then O'Neill and his friend Dr. Garzon decided to take a walk downtown towards the Gallows Café.

The two friends watched as a steady flow of sightseers streamed past the grove of hanging trees. There were all kinds of tourists - the new-born, young, mature and ancient, crawling, toddling, strutting and shambling, all staring stultified at the complexity of the ropes and levers and pulleys of the great mass-murder machine.

Tiny infants with round, horrified eyes were held up to view the fatal contraption.

O'Neill and Garzon overheard more than one parent remark, "That is what will happen to you, if you do not behave."

Small mouths opened up in horror, not understanding any of the subtle mechanics of the deathtrap contraption. But the clear message, do as you are told or it will be too bad for you, was instinctively understood.

O'Neill muttered to his friend, "The public gallows are a simple morality lesson."

It was twilight when people began to drift into the riverside cafes and beer gardens down near the town center.

At the Gallows Café, the locals were all deep in conversation about all the goings on in their town.

When O'Neill and Garzon came in, they decided to sit close by one of the tables and listen to what they were all talking about.   Maybe they would hear something of interest.

"You know Wilbur, I always had my suspicions about that Billies crowd up in the hills there," said one of the locals.

"Well, you never did saying nothing to me in that direction, Jim," said another.

"To be quite honest with you Wilbur, I was scared to.   That Driew family are weird, specially Big Billy. I don't know anyone around here who'd abeen brave enough to mess with him. Do you?"

"You're right there," said another voice putting in his twopence worth to the conversation.

"The weird clothes they all wore was enough for me," said Jim.

"And what about Big Billy always going on about his invisible pal 'Slim' – I think Big Billy must have been drinking some queer liquor or something. Did they have a still up there by any chance?" asked Wilbur.

"Not that I ever heard anything," said another voice. "They were all supposed to be religious or something."

"I don't know anyone that's ever been up to their place. In fact, I don't even know where their place is – come to think of it," said Jim.

"One thing's for sure," said Wilbur, "Maybe now we'll find out why some of the strangers who came into town never came back for their belongings."

"Yeah, I know what you mean, Wilbur," said another voice. "I hear that Ma Watson's boarding house has quite a lot of unclaimed stuff lying around in her storage shed."

"I've heard that the undertaker's been complaining about not been able to get workers," said Jim.

Suddenly another voice chipped in with an interesting piece of information that caught O'Neill's attention.

"What ever happened to that nice young couple, Simon and his wife that worked for him? My wife liked Jane or was it Jean? I think that was his wife's name. Anyway, Jean used to come over to our house and talk to Martha a lot about this and that."

"Well Pete, I heard that those two sisters that worked at the undertakers were always talking about some commune or other way back in the Greenwood Hills."

"Maybe they all cleared off to the commune together, who knows? Come to think of it, I also heard something else that might interest you'all," said Wilbur.

They all stared at Wilbur with querulous frowns. They were all ears.

"Well," continued Wilbur, "You must have noticed that old widow woman all in black who used to hang around with those two sisters. Seems that she's grandmaw Driew and she also calls herself the widow Vidova and she has some sort of commune up in the hills. What about that?"

They all shook their heads and looked at one another in astonishment.

"Well, I've asked around town and they all seemed to have disappeared," said Pete. "I've even heard rumors here and there that they mighta gone to some foreign parts or other."

"All I know is the undertaker is going crazy looking for extra help," said Jim.

The group all looked at each other and some stroked their chins as if to say, well I ain't going over there, are you.

Then the conversation changed track to something more in keeping with why they were all sitting in the café.

"Well I'm kindah hungry fellahs," said Wilbur, "I'm getting some grub and a large pitcher of iced tea. What about the rest of you guys?"

O'Neill heard all he needed to know. It certainly answered a few questions.

"Garzon, my friend, we've been doing a lot of asking around town and so far we haven't come across any potential cult members. I think all of the other members have disappeared with grandmaw Driew, maybe to some other country and I doubt if we'll ever find out where."

Garzon nodded in agreement.

Back in Dungowan

*

On the day the Driews were tried, that day in June, the courtroom of Judge Harkness smelt bad. How bad? Well, it was human bad which is somewhat worse than cow-bad. Let's just say the smell of that courtroom was to man what an old fashioned byre was to a cow, in other words, not all that nice.

O'Neill and Garzon feared the worst. They were concerned that most of the facts would be suppressed so as not to encourage copycats and in order to retain credibility for the effectiveness of law and order in the field. In other words to preserve the status quo - no new courts, judges, lawmen or vigilantes were wanted.

But by playing down the enormity of the crimes, much useful evidence would be lost, evidence that might have led to the flushing out or hunting down of the various members of the Cult of Vidova. Even the names of any witnesses, victims' families or places might have led to revealing the identity of other possible members.

The location of any communes yet

unidentified would have been a help. A death sentence on the accused, wiping out all these memories and potential clues, would be the worst outcome of all. Yet such a sentence was virtually certain.

O'Neill would argue for a sentence of guilty but insane and confinement for life in an asylum but with little hope of success.

O'Neill was despondent.

Hanging Judge Harkness could only hang people once and this he was very likely to do. It was for some of these reasons that Dr. Garzon was ill at ease in the courtroom of Hanging Judge Harkness.

The only clues to the wider existence, true purposes or present location of the Cult, were about to be destroyed. Death for the captured members would silence them forever. No one was ever reprieved from the ropes of the Hanging Judge so that no deal of clemency for information would ever be possible.

Garzon was despondent and felt the same way that he had when one of his carefully put together experiments had accidentally fallen and then drained dismally down the laboratory sink. Only worse, the chemical compound had been the work of days. This was the work of some years disappearing into the dark shadows of the hanging machine, yet what else could they have done to stop the rot of the Driews.

At times, the Hanging Judge seemed to be overwhelmed by the evidence, reacting to the demeanor of the accused or the evidence of witnesses with fierce, piercing glances, headshaking, raising of hands or the openmouthed glare of disbelief. At other times Judge Harkness listened pensively, almost as one in a trance.

"He's sincere, I'll certainly give him that," whispered Garzon, himself no lover of hangings.

O'Neill shook his head. "That's what I fear the most - people who are sincere but wrong. Vidova, wherever she may be, is sincere but not on the right path at all. I'm sure, as you know."

The judge limited the evidence to only a few possible crimes to spare the families of some of the victims and speed the work of the hangman.

At that moment, Judge Harkness was like the original hell-fire preacher, eager, hot-blooded and impatient.

By contrast, the jury sat like the frozen chosen in a Baptist Church gallery, stiff and scared looking and who could blame them? Weeping witnesses identified the buckles, watches, lockets, jewelry of long dead friends, neighbors and relatives. Fingers of fear pointed at the various members of the Driew clan who sat silently in the area of the courtroom reserved for the accused.

Judge Harkness finally yelled out to the jury, in his supposed to be impartial, judicial summing up, "Go from this courtroom and bring back the only verdict I will accept, the only verdict that will not set free the most vile and dangerous murderers that this courtroom has ever known."

When the jury filed out of the courtroom Garzon turned to O'Neill and whispered, "Felix, what do you think?"

"This is one of the few occasions when I totally agree with the outcome of law and order," said his friend.

He nodded his head and pointed emphatically with his right hand, "That's what I think."

***

Chapter 8
The Big Day Cometh

The citizenry of Dungowan were already beginning on the preparations for the day of the hangings.

"They certainly are hardworking folk in this town, Felix," Garzon remarked to his friend O'Neill. "Look at these high porches and balconies being filled with chairs, fronts being repainted, special platforms being built and I notice the store-keepers shelves being re-stocked."

Garzon pointed out to O'Neill that even soap, previously long treasured, was placed beside tubs and wash-hand basins.

"I would suggest that this may be an anticipated reenactment of the all too symbolic lavings of Pontius Pilate and ancient days," said O'Neill. "As always, a guilty exercise in handwashing must masquerade as justice and the clean witnesses of the dreaded scene would then be able to exult and rejoice in the efficacy of human justice."

"In short, these killings, legal and illegal, called for one big celebration," said Garzon.

"That's about it," concluded O'Neill.

However, after the trial of the Driews, Felix O'Neill slept badly that night in the Grand Hotel on the square in Dungowan.

When O'Neill awoke the next morning he remarked to Garzon, "I had a terrible night's sleep. What about you?"

"Not too bad. It took a while to doze off. What happened to you?"

"Demons seemed to walk the halls of this place last night and for some reason they visited me. Sleep is the highway of demons. By this road, demons leap into the mind and the soul of a man to mock and mislead him in dreams."

The sharp legal mind of O'Neill was having a hazy holiday, a day off in legalistic nightmares in which his drowsy mind struggled to reach the surface of meaning.

"There are dread dreams that are

shared by many and nightmares where hideous monsters flit and fleet and lope across that dreamscape unhindered by any boundary of time or space," he continued. "The sleeping mind is open to invasion by fiends that spring out of the void, leaping from dream to dream."

O'Neill was not in a good mood. It was a case of who would be next of kill?

"How could anyone have a calm night's sleep after that courtroom experience yesterday?" remarked Garzon.

O'Neill and Garzon sat by a window in the hotel and watched as the crowds poured into Dungowan.

"The coming event in a sense is apocalyptic," remarked Felix. "Indeed, all the persons involved are worthy of a seat of honor to view the unfolding of the battle of Armageddon itself."

"Indeed," agreed Garzon.

"If that great final battle between good and evil should ever occur, it would be necessary to have honest witnesses and spectators," concluded O'Neill.

"Well, the Driew clan are now well and truly on death row," replied Garzon.

Like vultures, even more visitors were swooping into Dungowan to see the soon-to-be public hanging as Felix O'Neill walked outside the hotel followed by Garzon. They looked around at the fairly busy town center before finding their new horses.

"Felix, we're still hearing of persons going missing mysteriously."

"This means, Garzon, that the Cult leaders have not been caught yet. This confirms what I suspected, that somewhere in these hills there is still a deadly Cult that real men and women disappear into - brainwashed or not?"

"But who or what or where are these cultists, Felix, like the widow Vidova?

"I wonder how many others have never received retribution in full for all their past blackmails and murders?" Felix mused.

"Yes indeed," added Garzon, "And I often wonder how it is possible for such debased, perhaps insane malefactors to live an outwardly respectable existence among decent people and, at the same time, lead a second and hidden life of murder and greed behind the curtains of convention. Are there more such perverts around than we have ever realized?"

"I bet there are," said O'Neill. "Do we ever find out about most of the secret crimes concealed behind the closed doors and shutters of unsuspected satancraft?

"Does this explain the occasional sudden disasters that befall some people so suddenly and sadly and are these disasters really crimes by close relatives and friends or are they in some cases retribution from an outraged moral eternity? We can only gape in horror. Who can tell?"

Garzon agreed.

The two friends rode out somberly through the hanging fair to look over the preparations for the coming stage-drama of destruction.

Felix reined in his horse to avoid collision with a handsome young couple dashing across the road and blind to all-comers.

Then he smiled, tipped his hat to the lady and remarked to Garzon, "Everybody is looking for romance. Some want to dream on - someone to care for, a true love.

"All I'm looking for is a chance to do a good job with this investigation."

He shook his head and lifted his eyes, "Is that too much to ask of life? Just so that I can buy a little cabin in the wooded hills up yonder and get as far away as possible from as many people as possible for as long as possible. Instead of a welcome mat, I'm going to post a notice on my front gate – **Keep Out. My Only Friend is a Shotgun.**"

Garzon laughed loudly, "Including me too, Felix?"

"Well," O'Neill relented, "Of course, present company excepted . . perhaps."

Garzon nodded, "In view of the judge's pageant play, it's understandable how you feel."

Felix nodded. "Well, we will get plenty of aloneness once we get back on the trail - it's just that these crowds get to you when you're used to solitary work."

"You're right, Felix."

"But still I'm serious about that hillwood cabin - just a plain old getaway - that's for me. How about you Garzon?"

Garzon smiled his usual closed-mouth sideways smile and nodded.

"Yes," he agreed, "Same here. Now I come to think of it, seems to me I've had just about the same idea myself more or less for some time."

The two partners had become loners from long trekking. Just what would it be like out there really, even for a little while, among the mobs? Would it be bearable? Probably not.

O'Neill remarked to Garzon, "It's a strange fact that when a hanging is to take place the weather is usually dull and cloudy."

"Is that so? I've never noticed that myself," responded Garzon.

"Yes indeed," continued O'Neill, "This fact has been reported many times and from various places all over the world. Once again, it seems that the creatures of mother earth that were made out of the soil are just a small part of one green organic machine."

"Perhaps the explanation is simpler," replied Garzon, "Maybe God wants to reserve capital punishment for His own day of the last judgment. Perhaps God does not like hangings."

O'Neill nodded to his friend, "Perhaps it's all part of a natural machine not a mechanical machine like the ones that man creates but a living machine where the various parts interrelate far more subtly and sensitively than is generally understood.

"When people enter the world of sleep with the intention of wakening up the next morning to hang one of their own kind whether justifiably or not, surely the collective mind of the earth is somehow informed of this grim intention and responds with a dull, deadly and dreary face. Indeed, nothing less would be acceptable from a living force of nature for surely it would seem odd. It would be crass to hang a man on a nice cheerful morning."

"Indeed, I see what you mean, Felix."

O'Neill continued with his friendly tirade, "If Nature said, Good morning, wake up folks, the sun is shining, the birds are bobbing and jumping and the flowers are singing, let's all go a-hanging today, what would we think of nature - Callous and insensitive at best, brutal and vicious at worst?

"But no. Nature says, Alas, let's weep. Here comes a sad event but we must bear with it. There's no avoiding it. Here's a dull day for hanging, so let's be business-like about it - a drab day for a dreary deed. That's what Nature says.

"But when man has his say he will have none of this - not at all. He says, let's be bright, let's dance and have a festival. The deed is necessary for our social good, so let's all have fun. The moral necessity to terminally torture the terrible malcreant must be celebrated with victorious and triumphal demonstrations. Aye, let's have fun and games and drinks all around. Eat, drink, and be merry for today a wretched scoundrel dies."

O'Neill and Garzon agreed that Judge Harkness was himself no party to any such judicial jamboreeism. He may have been unmerciful, legalistic and ruthless but Judge Harkness was no clown, no dolt; he was not insensitive. On the contrary, he was a servant of the law who was terrifying in his seriousness and his sensitivity.

"With death everything falls apart, Garzon."

"Everything? Is that so?" responded Garzon.

"That is a fact. Nothing lives and nothing survives when death enters the doorway. Death destroys everything but the soul. That is to say not only the physical life but the mental, the moral, the belief in God, the intellectual, the cultural, the family relationships, the community spirit - everything."

"That's a terrible thought, O'Neill."

"Did you know that some of the condemned make sounds of orthodoxy and faith in the hope of a reprieve?" said O'Neill.

"No, O'Neill, I've never that before."

"But in truth Death is the Destroyer of all," replied O'Neill, "including hope and faith."

But the crowds that came to Dungowan were not all there for vengeance or triumph or vicarious victory over the losers. Indeed, there were the occasional men and women of prayer, old and sifted.

Holy men and women gray
Who have for decades done nothing
  but pray
And there's nothing left there
Everything is drained away
But white hair
And prayer
Some old men came on sticks
Stumbling
Grumbling
And crumbling and mumbling
Slow, unfit, they keep on to see
One last uplifting sight
Before they too went tumbling
Into the pit

The motives for and against hanging that held forth here were the same as everywhere else. These were the old ones looking less than happy, mournful even, as if anyone could mourn the passing of the Driews. But maybe they mourned for something else, the crowd perhaps or humanity or the systems of justice of this world or the mills of God - so slow and mysterious even if efficacious in the end.

So the Driews were on death row.

The crowds came to see.

"Oh yes, excuse me sir."

"What?"

"Where is it?"

"Where is what?"

"The infernal hanging machine."

"Just off of Fortress Avenue, right near the jetty on the Old Snowy River. Just foller the crowds, ma'am."

As O'Neill and Garzon walked around the town among the crowds, O'Neill remarked, "A hanging is honest and public-spirited and a good example to show the kids what happened to bad folks."

They watched and listened as the evangelists told the people to hold up the scripture texts - perhaps one of the doomed would see and repent and trust in the Lord and see the light, even through the last window on life. Let's all sing a gospel song - Count Your Blessings or In the Sweet Bye and Bye.

For some, this was a family occasion. But there on the gallows stood several members of the most closely knit family of all, the Driews, who were dedicated to each other to the utter exclusion of any compassion towards anyone outside their lethal cult.

As the Driew's family took their last brief stroll together on thin air, hand clapping and the shouts of 'axe, axe, axe' were heard as Malmeurte's diabolical contraption swung into high gear. When those strange hosts of homicidal hospitality swung into eternity, their eyes rolled, they writhed and twisted and their tongues hung out with their faces black and blue.

A great roar went up from the crowd. It sounded like the shout of approval at a circus when a clever acrobat has swung into space and lived. But this time, killers would swing into space and die.

Here at the hanging grove, there was the cheer and enthusiasm of a grim wake but with the addition of a smug sense of superiority that some of the living feel over those who are about to be put to death for malfeasance.

One would wish that it could be said that the Driew malcreants had died with dignity. But no. Until the dark hoods of passing muffled their voices they had screamed and spat curses at the rabble and at the hangmen and at the tree-loving judge.

But the hangman's deputies did their work well and had bound the malefactors with cords as the mob had yelled and roared.

"Sling them and swing them."

"Heave them and leave them."

The trapdoors had opened and silence took over for that brief moment of terror.

Why the silence? What did the avid audience expect?

That the blackbirds in the hangman's tree would fly off to freedom?

That the flowers in the garden of doom would fail to fall to the gruesome gardener's scythe?

Slim chance. The trapdoor fell.

The bags of condemned carcasses - dropped like rejected meat into the swillbin of a slaughterhouse.

None of the birds flew away.

No miracle of reprieve took place.

The crowd broke silence and yelled its approval at the inevitable retribution of evildoers.

"A hanging in Dungowan is almost as

good as a camp gospel meeting," said Garzon. "I noticed placards like Jesus Saves and The Wages of Sin is Death held up high for the benefit of the doomed men."

"Perhaps a bit late," said O'Neill.

"I mentioned that to some of the evangelists, Felix, but they would have none of it. Remember the good thief at Calvary? They told me it was never too late to repent for a better life with Jesus in the next world - not even with a noose around your neck. It was a kindly thought."

***

Chapter 9
The Aftermath

As they sat by the riverside in Dungowan, O'Neill and Garzon had been thinking about the rights and wrongs of what had just taken place.

"Well I suppose I have no problem with hanging as long as they get the right man," commented Garzon dubiously. "I would worry if even once in a while we hanged the wrong man."

O'Neill responded sharply, "We hang the wrong man much more often than you think. So forget it. We might as well stop the hangings now rather than later. The next innocent men hanged wrongly in theory could even be us."

Then Garzon asked quietly, "Would it be all worth it to keep law and order and save even more lives?"

"Is what worth what Garzon?"

"All this Carnival of Hanging goings on here," as he pointed to the crowds mingling around town.

"Certainly Garzon, it's worth it alright when I think of the damage this Driew cult brought on dozens of helpless humanity - hundreds, if you count their widows and orphans - the Driews are just not fit to live. If they lived, they might escape from jail or outlive their sentences. Oh no - that would be too dangerous a possibility. The best outcome is death for people like the Driews. I have no problem with hanging them. What's the matter with you Garzon? Are you getting soft or something?"

"Maybe I am Felix because sometimes I wonder if we're not bringing ourselves down to their level by hanging them. You know, two wrongs don't make a right. Killing is always a wrong line of thought. I kind of agree with you in a way just so long as the sheriffs and the lawmen and the jury and the judge and the detectives keep their ambitions and their careers out of it and just go about catching the real villains then I can say go ahead and hang them - maybe.

"Well, I still think we should have

some doubts, Felix, if we didn't have doubts we'd really be as bad as the Driews. Look at the hanging Judge himself there - watching the fixings for the hangings - you can't see from here - but if you take a spyglass and looked at him closely as some have done - you'll see that more than likely he's weeping.

"Why's he doing that Felix?"

"He weeps because he has a hard task," responded O'Neill, "the task of judging for himself, who will live and who will die. He weeps for the fragility of life, for you, for me, for all of us. For one day we will all follow after the most cold-blooded killer, whether we end up in the same place or not. We've all got to leave this world one day. We're all mortal. We all die. The judge there is a middle-aged man, he knows he'll grow old and die pretty soon. My guess is that's why he weeps. But whether my guess is right or not, he is taking the whole matter seriously unlike most of the holidaymakers."

After thinking it all over Garzon conceded, "Well, I see what you mean. There's a lot of people make a lot of money and get started in politics, off of a good hanging. I guess it could be us one day for the high jump with a judge like that. Anyone could get on the losing side in this place. It's hang-happy."

However, O'Neill and his friend Garzon were lucky to escape such a fate and went on to pursue many another worthy quarry.

As O'Neill later remarked to Garzon, "Yes . . we survived but were never able to find again the rest of the secret circle. At least the worst of the clan were well and truly dead and the rest scattered. There were other survivors about whom we can only guess or vainly gather faint rumors.

"It would seem that our faithful dog Moro had no idea what was going on at the remote farmhouse but his dog sense must have told him it was nothing good. After a couple of disheartened howls he maybe loped forlornly back along the trail to lie down beside his second best pals, our horses Glory and Medallion - still waiting uneasily at the side of an abandoned path for us to return – which we never did.

"As far as the remote rumors tell, life

was not all bad for Moro and Medallion and Glory in their supposed new home somewhere but who can tell?"

Garzon was fascinated as O'Neill continued in his analysis of the cult.

"Later, it may be that an old woman would move into a large remote old farmhouse somewhere. She will have some relatives as helpers together with their young children. What could be more innocent than the presence of a close-knit family with young children?

"It is no wonder that children can be sold for half their weight in gold. They can certainly provide the perfect picture-cover for the forbidden guidebook to the most monstrous crimes against missing persons for they adore the old lady. She explains to them how they are all different from the people in the great secret societies - those manipulative people who rule the world are rich and powerful.

"In short, everything that brings the good life to men and women is controlled by the great circles that rule the world. You children have a choice, she tells them. You can enter the lottery that is life outside of the great circles that rule the world. Almost certainly you will lose, as with any lottery or you can grow up to be an insider.

"Perhaps far into the future the Circle members will practice their fatal trade with their blend of hospitality and homicide, suffering and slaughter. There is no telling where they might be or what they might do. Some may even be witty or attractive or intelligent or sophisticated, using poison and chemicals instead of guns and caves.

"Vidova may live on for many years and the Circle may have followers in many places. Veiled, she will still haunt graveyards for the bodies of the dead and those who mourn the dead. Wherever death dwells - there she will be. But when she waits in the rain and mourners come and go in groups and families she looks sideways and grows weary. Then she will take to the streets, the shadowy wayside eating houses, the dances, the churches or the clubs - wherever people meet - the lonely railway station or the religious retreat where people pray - she will appear to prey. Maybe she will even roam the hill, beloved of hill climbers or the solitary country inns, wherever unwary people may greet each other to find a friend.

"But most of all at funerals and wakes and graveyards there will be one who lurks behind, a waiting one who strangely lingers. She is the brokenhearted widow who is too overcome to leave - the one who may wear a veil. And yet who will know where such a stranger comes from or who or what she may be? And how many will there be like her?

"Have any gone missing in those parts of the world, Garzon, where you intend to travel in the course of your own professional activities?"

After a moment or two Garzon assured O'Neill that he did not intend to do so in the foreseeable future as he shook his head and spoke with a voice filled with finality.

O'Neill smiled understandingly, "My dear Garzon, after what we have both witnessed of the fate of so many I quite agree with you my friend.

"Anyhow, the breezes will still blow back and forth through bushes and among small creatures. The critters will cry out in their own sweet voices but neither you nor anyone else will hear them. Who or what were the birds, the shadows, the dark shades and shapes that flitted among those tumultuous green ocean of wooden hills and terrifying mountainous waves? Surely there must be some great treasures hidden in those far off byways, green but misted like a doorway to some earthly paradise?

"But we survived," said O'Neill.

"Yes, we did indeed although at times I thought we wouldn't make it. But we did," agreed Garzon.

"I feel sure we'll go on to follow other adventures, my friend" said O'Neill, "although it seems that the widow Vidova and her Cult also still survives and rules over her hidden commune in some unknown land."

THE END

Let the Lonely Traveler BEWARE!